JACKSON PEARCE & MAGGIE STIEFVATER

Pip Bartlett's

GUIDE TO

UNICORN TRAINING

SCHOLASTIC PRESS

ISBN 978-0-545-70929-3

10 9 8 7 6 5 4 3 2 1   17 18 19 20

Printed in the U.S.A.   23
First printing 2017

Book design by Christopher Stengel

Heeeeeeeeeyyyyyyyyyyyyyyy!

I was shoveling Greater Rainbow Mink poop.

This wasn't as bad as you might think. Greater Rainbow Minks only eat burnt sugar, so their poop literally smells like candy. (It's *not* candy, of course. It's very important to remember that no matter how good it smells, it's still poop.)

This Mink was the first Greater Rainbow Mink I'd ever met in person, but I knew a lot about them because they had a very long entry in my favorite book in the world, *Jeffrey Higgleston's Guide to Magical Creatures.*

It turned out that *knowing* a lot about an animal from a book was not the same thing as learning about an animal in person. For instance, it was one thing to read *Greater Rainbow Minks are agile climbers*. It was another thing to see an animal the size of a striped sock whipping up a wall like gravity doesn't matter. This was why it was amazing that I got to spend the summer with Aunt Emma

Greater Rainbow Mink

Native to South American rain forests, the Mink's vibrant colors allow it to easily hide among tropical flowers

This large Mink is friendly but food-driven; it has been known to knock down children & walls to get to candy

Eyes see approximately 8,000 times more colors than the human eye

Sugary hair provides a home to a variety of other nearly invisible species such as the SweetFlea

---

SIZE: 24-36" long
WEIGHT: 17 lbs. exactly
DESCRIPTION: Scientists have yet to discover how the Greater Rainbow Mink always weighs exactly 17 lbs. Its steady weight combined with its affinity for candy have made it an object of interest for companies that develop weight-loss products. No practical value has been found in the sugar-loving Greater Rainbow Mink, however, besides their intent affection.

at the Cloverton Clinic for Magical Creatures. I met a new animal *every day*.

"Sugar-*sugar*-sugar-*sugar*," shouted the Mink, running up and down the cage wall, tail flapping like a rainbow-colored flag. To everyone else in the world, her squeaks would've sounded random. But unlike anyone else in the world, I could understand and talk to magical creatures.

Darting to me, the Mink grabbed my pant leg with small furry fists. She shook it pleadingly. "Please? Please gimme sugar? I would like some sugar please please please sugar."

Sometimes understanding magical creatures isn't the most useful of skills.

"You've already had breakfast. You'll get more sugar at lunch," I told her.

"Sugar-sugar-sugar. Lunch sugar. Lunch sugar!" the Greater Rainbow Mink squealed. She released a small caramel-scented fart before leaping away.

Even though I wasn't climbing the cage walls like the Rainbow Mink, on the inside, I was just as excited. Because even though it seemed like a normal day at the Cloverton Clinic, it wasn't. Because today was the day before the Triple Trident.

I'd wanted to go to the Triple Trident ever since I found out about it, but it never worked out. My parents were

TRIPLE TRIDENT
CLOVERTON, GA

PREMIUM LIST
ALL-BREED
Entries are open to All UUSO Registered
Unicorns over Six Months of Age

Sponsored by
Cloverton Unicorn Club
(licensed by the United Unicorn
Show Organization)

Round One: Conformation — All Entries Appear in Ring
Round Two: Agility — All Entries Unless Disqualified for Physical Fitness
Round Three: Princess Round — All Entries Unless Disqualified for Temperment
Showground Hours: 8:30 A.M.-4:30 P.M.

All Unicorns must test negative for RainbowBeetles and Glitterlice.
All Unicorns and handlers must follow the rules of UUSO Sanctioned Shows.

geologists, and summer was a really busy time for them with travel. Plus, neither of my parents was animal-crazy. I knew they would've taken me if I'd begged, but it wouldn't have been fun for me, knowing they were actually secretly bored.

But now it was finally happening! The Triple Trident was right here in Cloverton. Aunt Emma loved animals. And I could go with my new friend Tomas. There'd be Unicorns and Griffins and Pegasi and Sallifourths and—

"Caramels! Butterscotch! Taffy!" shouted the Mink, grabbing her feet and rocking back and forth.

"*I know!*" I shouted back, equally excited, even if it was about something totally different.

We peered at each other. I could see myself in the Mink's beady, adorable eyeballs. I wondered if she could see herself in mine.

A loud, low voice made us break our touching eye contact.

"Heyyyyyyyyyyyyyyyy!!"

I asked the Mink, "Did you hear that?"

"Lollipops and gumdrops and gummies!"

That seemed like a no.

"Heyyyyyyyyyyyyyyyy!!" The voice blasted again. This time I could tell it was coming from outside the clinic's back door. It sounded like a magical creature to me, which was strange, because normally I could understand more of what they were saying. But this one just sounded like—

"Heyyyyyyyyyyyyyy!!!"

"Don't pull!" *This* voice was a human voice for sure, sounding sharp and concerned.

"Stay here," I told the Mink, slipping her a caramel from my pocket ("sugar-*sugar*-sugar-*sugar*") and carefully letting myself out of her cage. I hurriedly scrubbed my hands in the back-room sink (it's important not to transfer any magical sicknesses from animal to animal) and pushed open the door.

The Georgia summer, hot and sticky, hit me first, and then the sound—"Heyyyyyyyyyyyyyy!"—hit me second.

In the side lot beside the clinic, Aunt Emma stood as if she was ready to catch a football. Legs braced. Arms wide. It took a lot to fluster her, but she looked as close to flustered as she got. Her short hair stuck up sweatily in all directions, with just one lock—the one she'd dyed pink—pasted over her forehead. Another lady in overalls stood about ten feet away, right in front of a pickup truck and tidy small livestock trailer.

This lady had definitely crossed over the flustered line. She was also *not* throwing a football. She was holding one end of a rope leash; the other end was attached to a collar that hovered midair.

"Pip," Aunt Emma said in a very level voice, "keep your voice quite calm. We're dealing with a Rockshine."

"Oh!" I started to exclaim—but then I clapped a hand over my mouth. Rockshines are a species of Glimmerbeast. They're farm animals, so I hadn't run across any in the big city of Atlanta. But I remembered two important facts from their entry in the *Guide to Magical Creatures*:

1. They went invisible when they were excited or alarmed.
2. They were not very smart.

Clearly this Rockshine was very excited or alarmed, because it was completely invisible, which was why the leash ended in . . . nothingness.

A sound erupted from the empty air between Aunt Emma and the other lady: "Heyyyyyyyyyyyyyy!"

I had thought that I might be able to figure out what the creature was saying once I was closer, but now I realized that when the Rockshine said, "*Heeyyyyyyy!*" it meant: *Hey!* Or maybe *Hay!*

"What can I do?" I asked Aunt Emma.

Rockshine

Like all Glimmerbeasts, the Rockshine has the ability to flicker between visibility and invisibility

Not particularly intelligent

Not particularly active or agile

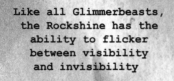

Not particularly bad-tempered

Not particularly difficult to raise, though collars are necessary due to their invisibility

Not particularly difficult to feed; Rockshines will eat grass, trash, straw, wood, rocks, mulch, and, if pressed, dirt

---

SIZE: 36" at shoulder
WEIGHT: 40-50 lbs.
DESCRIPTION: The most common variety of Glimmerbeast, the Rockshine is the distant domesticated descendant of Tibet's Imperial Invisible Ibex. Originally, farmers hoped to create invisibility cloaks from Rockshine wool, but the wool becomes visible once sheared.

In a smooth, soothing voice, my aunt said, "Callie went to get some carrots. We're hoping that will cheer him up enough that he'll become at least partially visible."

I wanted to ask why they didn't just put him back in the trailer, even if he was invisible, but I didn't want to risk talking too much and scaring him further. Luckily, the woman in overalls explained, "His collar is too loose. It's my own fault—I grabbed the wrong one on the way out the door. He's just about pulled out of it, though, and if he does, we'll never find him!"

I kept my voice low. "Is there a way to tighten the collar?"

"Not without taking it off," said the lady.

"And we don't have a collar big enough for him," Aunt Emma said. "I checked."

I had an idea. One of my jobs at the clinic was walking Bubbles, a cranky Miniature Silky Griffin. He didn't wear a collar because Aunt Emma didn't want him leaning his full weight against his neck. Instead, he wore a harness that strapped around his chest and legs. Bubbles was a *miniature* Griffin, so obviously his harness would be too small for a Rockshine, but . . .

"HEEEEEYYYYYYY!!!!" the Rockshine shouted again. I was beginning to think it meant *Hey, I will never be visible again!*

"Could we put that Standard Griffin harness on him? The one for the pup, I mean," I asked. Standard Griffins are big as horses, but their pups are about the size of a Rockshine. Like Bubbles, they wear harnesses too, but not to protect their throats. Their necks are just about the same size as their heads, so it's easy for a badly trained Griffin pup to slip out of its collar as it flies into the air. We didn't have a Griffin pup in the clinic, but I remembered that an old Griffin pup harness hung on the hook behind Bubbles's harness.

Both the lady and Aunt Emma looked at me like I was an ice-cream cone on a hot day. It actually made me a little nervous. People being very annoyed or very happy with me had the exact same effect.

"That's a great idea, Pip," Aunt Emma said. "I forgot we still had that red one. Yes, please go get that harness— quietly, if you can."

By the time I'd reemerged, my older cousin Callie had come outside as well. She was tall and skinny like Aunt Emma, but she had very long hair that she curled every day, just in case a director or Broadway producer saw her and thought, *There she is! The perfect star for our new musical, working the desk at a magical creature clinic!*

Right now Callie looked more furious than famous. Her

hair was already wilting in the Georgia heat. She held up the bucket of carrots—it looked like a bucket of fat fingers—and growled, "Tell me what I'm doing with these root vegetables so that I can go die in the air-conditioning."

"Here's the plan," Aunt Emma said. "Callie, you hold the bucket in the direction of the Rockshine's head—no, that's his butt. The other end. Mariah, wait till we see the carrots vanishing, then we'll know he's distracted and you can grab hold. Once you've got him, I'll put the harness on. Pip, stand back. He's not *that* big, but you aren't either, and he could knock you down."

There was a brief scuffle.

When everyone stopped moving, the lady was holding a glowing blue leg, Aunt Emma was fastening the last harness buckle, and Callie was eating a carrot as she headed back into the clinic.

The lady in the overalls wiped her hand on them and offered it to me to shake.

"Mariah Gould," she said. "Nice to meet you. Strong common-sense thinking there!"

We shook hands.

"Pip Bartlett," I said. And then, a little louder, "Pip *Bartlett*." I was trying to get better at talking to people, but it was still easier to talk to magical creatures.

"This is my niece," Aunt Emma said. She sounded proud. "She's here for the summer. Pip, Mariah's here for the Triple Trident."

"Hopefully, Bucky here is too," Ms. Gould said. "I just smelled a little bit of honey-breath from the herd today and wanted to make sure they were tested for Sweet Pox before we took them onto showgrounds."

"Aren't invisible animals hard to show?" I asked.

Ms. Gould nodded. "They have to be kept very calm. Total invisibility during a show is grounds for disqualification."

"Wow!" I said, picturing a whole pen full of invisible animals in harnesses.

"Perhaps you can help us out, Pip. We could use someone like you, with your *strong common-sense thinking*!" She said it in such a way that I could tell she said *strong common-sense thinking* a lot. "How about it?"

"Sure!"

Aunt Emma beamed at me. Callie wasn't very interested in magical creatures, so I knew Aunt Emma was extra-glad that I was.

The Rockshine was slowly becoming more and more visible. He was bigger than I'd expected, with thin legs and a round body that was covered in wispy beige hair. He had a short stubby snout and ears that flopped over into neat triangles. Like a pig-sheep-dog-thing. He was so ugly that he was sort of cute.

Sort of.

"There you are, my handsome boy," Ms. Gould said. "Thanks so much, Emma. And Pip! We'll see you at the Trident? Come find me in the Glimmerbeast section."

I grinned at her and patted Bucky's head. "I'll be there!"

It would take a pack of wild Grims to keep me away from the Triple Trident.

CHAPTER

2

Everyone Likes Chips

The Triple Trident was being held just outside of Cloverton at the county fairgrounds, which turned out to be a collection of outdoor rings and giant warehouse-type buildings. A huge banner read: THE 34TH ANNUAL TRIPLE TRIDENT. Pictures of Unicorns with glorious pink manes reared on either side of the letters.

My friend Tomas and I peered out the car window as Aunt Emma parked in front. Tomas sat in the backseat with me, a tissue already clutched in his right hand. He was allergic to most magical creatures, and *thought* he was allergic to the rest of them. Right now, for instance, he was wearing a giant bright blue backpack full of emergency supplies. He was already pretty small, and the backpack made him look even smaller. But Tomas liked to be prepared. And I liked that he didn't let his allergies keep him from having adventures.

Aunt Emma turned the car off. "Callie, would you look in the, ah, thingy, for the parking pass?"

"Gross!" Callie said as she flipped open the glove box. "I'm going to get black stuff all over my hands." The inside of the glove box was full of partially burned car manuals and receipts—the only sign remaining of the Fuzzle infestation we'd just dealt with.

"At least there isn't still a Fuzzle in there too," Tomas said grimly.

"Small blessings!" Aunt Emma declared, slapping the parking pass on the dash so that it was visible from outside of the car. "Everyone out!"

As we climbed out of the car, the scent of lavender— which was used for Unicorn bedding—whipped through the summer breeze. The parking lot was crammed full of livestock trailers, and underneath the hum of traffic and conversation were the squeaks, barks, squawks, and *aahh-oooo*s of dozens of magical creatures.

My heart thumped with excitement.

"Tomas," I whispered, "we're really here."

Tomas silently placed his inhaler in his mouth and took a solemn puff.

"We're really here," he echoed.

Beside us, Callie used the car window to study her

reflection. I was surprised that she'd so eagerly agreed to come—her interest in magical creatures was usually limited to keeping them from interfering with the rest of her life as much as possible. But not only had she come without complaining, she'd taken up the bathroom for almost two hours getting ready. She'd even tied a flower up in her hair and was carrying a purse made out of a Shakespeare book.

"Ready for battle?" Callie asked.

"Yeah!" I replied.

Callie looked surprised that I had answered. She'd been talking to her own reflection.

But it was true that she wasn't the only one prepared for battle. Tomas and I had spent hours going over the map of the arena, deciding which route meant maximum magical-creature time.

"Now, hey, you three," Aunt Emma said, two boxes stacked in her arms. "Don't go running off just yet. I need your help bringing the stuff for the booth."

Callie groaned, predictably. Tomas looked nervous, predictably. I looked longingly at the animal arena. Predictably.

"Soon, Pip," Aunt Emma promised. She loaded us down with supplies for the Cloverton Clinic for Magical Creatures booth—loading Tomas down slightly less than Callie and me, since he was already trudging under his backpack.

It was even *more* exciting inside the booth setup area. People scurried about with magical animal supplies. Animal sounds were everywhere. In the rafters overhead, Blankbirds flitted about.

"Ugh!" Callie said, as one swept perilously close to the flower in her hair.

"Look at them!" Aunt Emma said. We did. "Let's see if they'll do their thing—oh, there!"

As we watched, one of the darker Blankbirds opened its beak and projected a rainbow beam of light onto one of the white Blankbirds. Only it wasn't a rainbow once it hit the white feathers: All of the colors combined to create a picture of an open bag of chips on the bird's body.

"Male Blankbirds communicate by projecting images onto the females," Aunt Emma said, shuffling her boxes to her other hip for balance. "Looks like he's telling her about a bag of chips someone tossed on the ground. Blankbirds are very food motivated."

I could tell. Everyone else just heard the male Blankbird chirping madly, but I could understand what he was saying: "Honey! Look! There's a *bag of chips*! If we hurry now, we can beat the rush! *Go go go chips chips chips!*"

"I guess everyone likes chips," I said. "That was so much cooler than it was described in the *Guide*!"

Blankbird

Common in urban areas, Blankbirds enjoy varied diets of seeds, fruit, insects, and discarded human food

The male Blankbird's heart constantly creates a glow of light that projects when he opens his beak

Long flight feathers make the Blankbird an agile and acrobatic flyer

SIZE: 6-10"

WEIGHT: 6 oz.

DESCRIPTION: The males of this remarkable species have a truly photographic memory and are equipped with the ability to project remembered images onto any light-colored surface, including the white-feathered females. They use this method to communicate food sources in both rural and urban areas.

"I know," Aunt Emma replied, grinning. My copy of the *Guide* actually used to be Aunt Emma's, back when she was in vet school. "Maybe you can fix that later. Okay, let's go!"

We lugged the stuff to the booth, getting thoroughly sweaty and covered in a thin film of lavender dust in the process.

"I'm going to go find a bathroom to wash off my hands," Callie said, staring at her palms. She started to pat her hair, and then pulled her hand back in distaste. "If there is even a bathroom in a place like this."

Tomas said—a little stuffily, since he was allergic to all the lavender—"I saw a hose on the way in."

"A *hose*? I am not *livestock*!"

Tomas shrank behind me so that only his blue backpack stuck out.

"Don't shout," Aunt Emma told Callie. "The restrooms are down there. Also, there's nothing wrong with livestock."

With a muffled scream, Callie stomped off.

"It's safe," I told Tomas.

He reemerged with a little fan attached to a water bottle in his hand. He used it to mist his face before offering it to me.

"I'm okay," I said. "I don't mind being sweaty as long as I'm not smelly."

"I'll tell you if you start to smell," Tomas said helpfully. "You don't, yet."

We both turned to watch a tall man leading a Giant Sallifourth by us. Its enormous nose dragged on the ground as it walked, and it made a snuffling noise in my direction. It swept its nose the other direction and vacuumed up a candy wrapper with a little coughing, snotty sound. It swept its nose the other way and suctioned up a broken potato chip. It looked pleased.

"Wow," said Tomas, in a voice that suggested that he really meant *Yuck*.

"Everyone likes chips," I said again. "Aunt Emma, can Tomas and I go look around now?"

"Yes! Go! Go—oh, hey! You should go say hi to Mr. Henshaw at some point," Aunt Emma said.

"Mr. Henshaw?" I echoed. I guess I shouldn't have been *that* surprised that he was here. He was a client at the clinic—his nervous Unicorn, Regent Maximus, was a frequent patient. I supposed if he owned a Unicorn, it made sense that he'd be interested in watching the biggest Unicorn show in the state. I didn't really know what I'd say to him without Regent Maximus around, though.

Maybe just my usual nervous wave. "I guess I can ask how Regent Maximus is doing," I told Aunt Emma.

"You can see for yourself," she said. "The Unicorn is here."

"*What?*" Tomas and I asked at the same time.

Aunt Emma frowned up at both of us, as if our reaction confused her. "He's entered in the Trident, of course."

"*Regent Maximus?*" Tomas asked, shocked.

"Of course!" Aunt Emma laughed a little. "Regent Maximus *is* a show Unicorn! What did you expect?"

Tomas and I looked at each other.

We certainly hadn't expected *this*.

The Ideal Unicorn and How to Spot Him

Tomas and I *knew* Regent Maximus.

Even though Regent Maximus was a show Unicorn, I didn't really think that Regent Maximus was a Unicorn for *showing*. Jeffrey Higgleston, the author of the *Guide to Magical Creatures*, was an enormous Unicorn fancier, and the *Guide* dedicated a very long section to Unicorn types. At the beginning of the section, Higgleston described "the ideal Unicorn and how to spot him."

That was not what Regent Maximus looked like.

Shortly after I came to Cloverton, Regent Maximus's stable had burned down in an unfortunate Fuzzle incident, so he'd come to stay at the clinic. Tomas and I had tried to teach him to be less fearful, and I guess we'd made a little progress. Enough, it seemed, to convince Mr. Henshaw that his Unicorn might be able to make it through the Triple Trident.

I was not so convinced.

The Ideal Unicorn and How to Spot Him

Piercing stare

Horn is harder than diamonds

Bulletproof skin

The ideal Unicorn always carries head high

Tail color dictated by genetics and diet; the ideal Unicorn's tail color is pure and vibrant, never muddy

Ideal Unicorn lifts knees high in every gait

The ideal Unicorn is a thing of joy and wonder, a marvelous combination of elegance and performance that is unmatched in the animal kingdom. He is proud, poised, agile. He protects his tender beauty with a horn that can reach three feet long and up to forty pounds. This weight does not bow the head of the ideal Unicorn, however, as he is a tireless and fearless companion eager to defend both himself and his herd. The ideal Unicorn is horse-like, perhaps, in appearance, but lion-like in his brave heart.

If Jeffrey Higgleston had created a *Guide* page for Regent Maximus, it would have looked quite different.

"I can't believe Mr. Henshaw thinks Regent Maximus can do this," Tomas muttered as we walked through the arena, studying the map to find our way to the Unicorn area.

"Me ne—" I started. "Tomas, your hair!"

The first of Tomas's allergic reactions was apparently hitting him. His normally floppy black hair was slowly beginning to go super-light and floaty at the ends. Reaching a hand up, he patted it with a sigh.

"Hadgebadgers," he said grimly.

I eyed his head. It looked like a dandelion in full seed. "Do you need to take something for it? Will it kill you?"

"It could be worse," he replied. "Beebugs make my hair fall *out*."

Tomas did his best to dampen his hair with his mist bottle and slime it down with his hand. It only made it more impressive when his hair stood back up again, because now it looked like his head was covered with black plastic flames.

"Um?" I said.

"I'm good," he insisted.

I watched the last of his hair stand up and decided not to say anything more. If he was good, he was good.

Regent Maximus and How to Spot Him

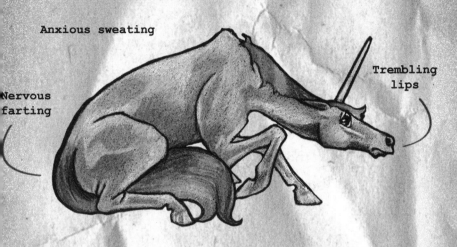

Anxious sweating

Trembling lips

Nervous farting

Lovely tail is permanently tucked between legs

Prefers to ooze or creep instead of trot or mince

Regent Maximus is a thing of fear and anxiety, a quivering combination of productive caution and paralyzing uncertainty. He was sold to Mr. Renshaw as a show Unicorn and came with a dazzling pedigree of ancestors who had dominated the Unicorn showing scene before him. His fear prevented him from even being led out in public places until his stable burned to the ground and he had to come spend time at the Cloverton Clinic for Magical Creatures, where Pip Bartlett and Tomas Ramirez helped him at least appear in public as long as he was wearing a blindfold to keep scary things from appearing in his field of vision.

We walked on. The booths were full of cool things for magical creatures—Giant Salamander collars, All-Weather Coats for winged mammals, spray glitter, and Unicorn hair tint. After the booths, there were dozens of rings with fancy little white fences that only came up to our waists. Competitions for some of the smaller magical creatures had already begun inside some of them.

I stopped to watch.

"What are those?" Tomas asked. His eyebrows were standing up now too, which I hadn't even known was possible.

"Patched LavaPets, I think?" I said. They looked like rocks, but when their handlers gave a command, little legs appeared from beneath them. A judge watched with crossed arms from the middle of the ring.

It was so exciting. I leaned over the fence to get a better look—

"Regent Maximus," Tomas reminded me.

We headed on. We passed Miniature Silky Griffins with their flowing coats, Llamadors with curly spotted fur and long necks, and finally a whole pen of Hugpuggles discussing how to take over the funnel-cake stand.

I could tell that we were getting closer to the Unicorn area as the fences got taller. The creatures behind them were getting taller too. Standard Griffins, Pegasi,

Bricksnouts, and, of course, Unicorns. Light streamed in over glistening manes and swishing tails as the Unicorns sauntered out of trailers and into the arena holding their silk-wrapped horns up high. One tossed its mane in my direction, pleased with how pretty it knew it was. I rolled my eyes. Unicorns are such show-offs.

Tomas and I craned our necks, trying to get a glimpse of Regent Maximus. It turned out that we shouldn't have been looking. We should have been *listening*.

A shout rang out above the hum of the show. Nearby Unicorns flicked their ears this way and that as their handlers turned to see where the commotion was coming from.

Then:

CRASH!

"My!" said one of the Unicorns closest to us. (It sounded like a surprised whinny to everyone else.)

BANG!

"What!" said another Unicorn. (A noisy snort.)

Finally, the high reedy voice of an animal cried out, "The walls are closing in! The trailer is shrinking! Help! Save me! *I PERISH AS A TUNA IN A CAN!*"

I sighed.

That was definitely Regent Maximus.

The handlers in the ring tried to quiet their own

Unicorns, thinking they were noisy because they were frightened. They were *not* scared, though; they were gossiping. The other humans heard only whinnying and screeching, but I heard:

"How embarrassing!"

"Why even *come* if you're going to act like such a filly?"

"Don't be ridiculous—I've had four fillies and not one of them has acted like *him*."

"I hear he was supposed to be famous, you know. Excellent bloodlines."

"Just proves it's not all about family. Star quality is a gift, not a birthright."

Feeling bad for Regent Maximus, I hissed to the closest Unicorn, "Don't pretend that you've never been scared!"

The Unicorn blinked its long lashes at me in shock, but I didn't have time to see if it had taken my words to heart. Regent Maximus was shrieking from the distance, "*No!* No, don't come in here! The oxygen is getting low! *HOLD YOUR BREATH!*"

"We should go see what we can do," I told Tomas.

"Should we?" Tomas asked.

"He won't understand anyone else!" I replied.

"Fine, fine, fine," Tomas said. "I brought first-aid cream."

We darted through people and animals until we recognized Mr. Henshaw's truck and trailer. Voices came from inside it. Hooves rapped urgently on its floor. Lavender bedding puffed out the tiny windows in hazy purple dusty clouds.

Tomas hiccuped, and a big turquoise-colored bubble came out of his mouth—he was allergic to Unicorns, and I guessed there were too many here for his medication to totally fix it.

The clattering of hooves grew even more frantic. Then the trailer door swung open with a monumental clank. There was Regent Maximus. His body was pure white. His mane and tail were every color of the rainbow. His horn gleamed like the inside of an oyster shell. The skin inside his nostrils was a deep, pure purple.

He was the glowing portrait of Jeffrey Higgleston's Ideal Unicorn.

Except for his eyeballs, which were bulging with terror.

"Regent Maximus!" I called.

"I HEAR DEATH CALLING MY NAME!" Regent Maximus screamed. He reared up, nearly punching his horn through the trailer roof. Tomas leaped behind a hay bale.

I held my hands up, trying to catch Regent Maximus's

attention, but he wasn't really looking at anything for long. He was tossing his head back and forth, blinking rapidly, when his mane got caught in his eyelashes. And he kept half rearing.

"Whoa! Get down!" Mr. Henshaw shouted over and over. It didn't do anything to calm Regent Maximus down, but I didn't blame Mr. Henshaw—Regent Maximus was terrifying when he was like this. His gaze landed on Tomas, where he was still huddled by the hay bale. Tomas's hair stood up in furious black spikes, his eyebrows bristled strangely above his eyes, and an assortment of red and purple bubbles popped from his mouth. His blue backpack made a hunch of his back.

Regent Maximus stared at the backpack. He was terrified of many things. Especially the color blue.

The backpack pushed him over the edge.

"TURTLE! BUBBLING DEATH-TURTLE!" Regent Maximus screamed. "I'M TOO YOUNG TO DIE!"

Mr. Henshaw snatched for his halter, but Regent Maximus jostled him into the trailer wall.

"FORGIVE ME! SAVE YOURSELVES!" howled Regent Maximus. He sprang.

Suddenly, I found the ideal Unicorn charging straight toward *me*.

CHAPTER 4

The Ideal Unicorn and How to Stop Him

Tomas yanked me out of the Unicorn's path.

Just in time too, because Regent Maximus didn't even pause. He charged right over the spot I had just been standing in, dust billowing up under his hooves. He wheeled to a halt in front of a display of fancy bridles, eyes rolling as he desperately searched for a new path. He sprinted off again.

I didn't know how to stop him. I only knew I had to try.

I took off after him. Tomas was on my heels, surprisingly fast given his enormous backpack and how many bottles of contact lens solution he'd crammed in the pockets of his cargo shorts. In front of us, people were shouting and pulling children and show animals out of Regent Maximus's way. He leaped nobly over boxes of Biddle Biddle food and smashed right through cages full of furry Snakelegs. Behind us, voices lifted—more and more people were joining us, eager to either stop the runaway Unicorn or see how the chase ended.

It felt weirdly backward. Before I'd come to Cloverton, I'd been involved in a Unicorn stampede—okay, I'd *caused* a Unicorn stampede—and it had felt a lot like this. Only this time, the people far outnumbered the Unicorns.

"Noooooooooooooooooooo," howled Regent Maximus as he soared over a pair of old women sitting in portable chairs. It was hard to tell what he was saying no to.

And it was hard to tell how long he'd keep running.

As we pursued him, other animals joined in. But only briefly. Curly-Coated Manticores and TriColored Llamadors broke free from their handlers and trotted, minced, and galloped with us on the other side of the competition fences, pulling up short when they reached the opposite side of the pen. We had a constantly rotating selection of animals lumbering or floating beside us.

At the front of the building, Regent Maximus was faced with the choice of bursting through the glass doors to the parking area or turning around.

For a moment, I was really worried he was going to choose the glass doors.

And for another moment, I hoped that the chase was over.

But instead, he spun, his hooves making sparks on the

GAITS OF FANCY
NORTH AMERICAN LIVESTOCK

LLAMADOR

STRIDE

TROT

GREEN-TIPPED PIXTON

CURLY-COATED
MANTICORE

GALLUMPH

concrete entrance floor. He crashed into the Llamador pen, sending fence bits flying.

"Pointy horse!" the Llamadors screamed.

"Furry Unicorns!" Regent Maximus cried. Instead of crashing through the other side of the tall Llamador pen, he leaped over the six-foot-high fence. I had to admit, he looked elegant, soaring through the air with his rainbow-colored mane and tail waving behind him.

The elegance vanished when he landed, because he knocked right into a man holding a red Slurpee. The drink leaped out of the cup and splattered on Regent Maximus's chest like a spray-paint butterfly.

"I'M HIT!" screamed Regent Maximus.

The adults in pursuit took the opportunity to split into two groups on either side of him, hoping to cut him off no matter which direction he turned to next. The only problem with that plan was that on one side was a ring full of Green-Tipped Pixtons, all trotting with their beaks held high, shells rocking back and forth as they moved. And on the other was a long line of Miss Triple Trident Tiara contestants in giant fluffy dresses.

"Turtle-monsters," Regent Maximus whimpered, looking at the Pixtons. He swung his head toward the beauty queens. *"Dresses!"*

He wasn't going to take on either of these threats. His

only option was to charge between the obstacles, back toward me.

And we'd already figured out that I wasn't enough to stop him.

I looked around. *Think, Pip, think!*

Regent Maximus charged. *No more time to think!*

Right next to me was a man dressed in a very nice suit with alligator-green shoes and a wide striped scarf wrapped around his neck. He looked confused by all the ruckus.

"Excuse me, sir, but it's an emergency!" I said.

Jumping up, I yanked the scarf off him. I did it so suddenly that he pinwheeled his arms and fell backward into a display of Pegasus leg wraps, but I didn't have time to apologize—Regent Maximus was almost upon me.

I tossed one end of the scarf to Tomas, who understood what I was thinking. We'd done this before, sort of.

Scrambling up onto two wobbly booth tables, we held the scarf high over our heads, right at Unicorn eye level.

When he saw the silky obstacle, Regent Maximus tried to stop, but it was no use. He was going too fast, and the floor was concrete here. He slid face-first into the scarf. The ends pulled from our hands, but the fabric fluttered around his ears, kept in place by his horn. It covered his eyes entirely.

With matching triumphant grins, Tomas and I leaped off the tables.

The Unicorn took a few more panicked steps, knees shaking. Then he slowed, slowed, slowed. Finally, he simply stood with his knees knocking together. He was making little blubbering noises with his lips.

"Regent Maximus! It's Pip!"

"Phhhbbbbtpip? PhhhbbbtPip?" He blew slobbery, nervous bubbles out of his nose as he dropped his head down by mine.

"Don't run, okay?" I said.

"Is it still *blue* out there?" Regent Maximus asked, voice trembling.

"Kind of," I said, because I couldn't bring myself to lie. "But you're safe."

"I can't believe this," Mr. Henshaw gasped. He had finally reached us, huffing and puffing. He stepped out of the group of other grown-ups, looking out of place. He was dressed fancily, like for a business meeting, while the others wore shirts that read things like STARLIGHT CATTERY and FIZZLETON UNICORN TRAINING. It seemed like we'd picked up someone from each and every ring or stall we'd dashed past or through or over.

"Quick thinking, kiddo!" a bearded man said.

"Glad we caught him," a woman agreed.

"I've got a lead rope, if you need it to walk him back!" someone in the back called.

The only person who wasn't smiling was Mr. Henshaw, who looked both humiliated and frustrated. He kept shaking his head, as if Regent Maximus was a question and he didn't want to answer.

"Are you all right, Pip?" he asked.

"Yeah," I answered, even though I knew it didn't look like it. Tomas was applying a Band-Aid to a minuscule scratch I'd gotten somewhere in the midst of it all.

When I tried to brush him off, Tomas slapped my hand away. "You don't want it to get infected! Flesh-eating bacteria has been experiencing a resurgence in Georgia."

"I'm so sorry," Mr. Henshaw said. "I feel terrible that this happened. I tried blindfolding him, but it didn't work like that for me! He just panicked more! I just don't know how to handle him, Pip."

"Well, Regent Maximus and I have a little history," I said kindly. I didn't want him to feel bad—it wasn't his fault he couldn't talk to magical creatures, after all.

Mr. Henshaw blinked at the scarf as if just noticing it. "Where did that come from?"

"Oh . . . um . . ." I turned around toward the man I'd stolen it from. He was only now clambering out of the Pegasus leg wraps. Little sticky bits of the wrap tape were fixed to his clothes, and his hair seemed out of place. Actually, it *was* out of place—he had a fake hairpiece covering up a sizable heart-shaped bald spot on the back of his head.

I pointed. "That guy. The one with the wig."

"It's actually called a *toupee*—wait." Mr. Henshaw's eyes narrowed, then went wide. "*That* man gave you the scarf?"

He sounded so dismayed that I stammered. "Well . . . sort of. I had to think fast."

"Oh dear," Mr. Henshaw said as the scarf-man started toward us. "This can only make things worse!"

"Why? What's wrong? Who is he?" Tomas asked in a whisper.

Mr. Henshaw didn't have a chance to answer, because the scarf-man was upon us. His jaw was square and firm. His toupee was glistening and bushy. His clothing, even under the bits of leg wraps, was expensive-looking. He was Jeffrey Higgleston's Ideal Man.

Except for his piercing and narrowed green eyes, fixed right on us.

He cleared his throat.

"Excuse me, miss. I'm Prince Temujin, and I believe that Unicorn"—the man paused to point toward Regent Maximus—"is wearing my scarf."

CHAPTER 5

Feels Like Home. Suspiciously Like Home.

"Prince?" I echoed, eyes wide. I'd never met a real prince, but I thought they had crowns. Or white suits. Or—I wasn't sure. I didn't think they just appeared in the middle of Unicorn shows in places where girls could accidentally shove them into Pegasus-leg-wrapping booths. It didn't seem very *royal*.

"Pip," Mr. Henshaw said quite awkwardly, "Prince Temujin is here to judge the Unicorn competition. His great-great-great-great-grandmother was the first princess to tame a Unicorn. You know the story, I'm sure."

I did know that story! *Everyone* did!

"Oh!" I said.

At the same time, Tomas sank into a deep bow.

"Your Majesty," he said respectfully, as tubes and tubes of lip balm rolled out of his shirt pocket and onto the floor.

My face was quite red. I said quickly, my words

Once upon a time, all of the Unicorns were wild. They lived in the fields and mountains, keeping to themselves, only appearing sometimes to gore villagers with their pure horns. So secretive and savage were they that no one managed to tame them until 1523, when Princess Albreda had a prophetic dream. In the dream, a Unicorn appeared to her and told her that Unicorns enjoyed both harp music and cheese crackers.

On waking, Albreda approached the herd outside her castle with both of these things. The young Unicorns were the first to be lured, and the rest of the herd soon followed. This is why Albreda is often called the Mother of Unicorns and also why many brands of cheese crackers are named after her.

stumbling over one another, "I'm sorry about your scarf, sir. I didn't know it was yours. I mean, I knew it was *yours*, but I didn't know you were a prince. I thought it was just an ordinary-person scarf—"

"It's all right, it's all right. Though it is printed with the flag of my country, so if I could get it back . . ." Prince Temujin trailed off, his gaze flitting over Regent Maximus. The Unicorn was sucking on the long end of the scarf, his lips quivering as they smacked against the fabric. Drool dripped down the fabric and onto the floor in front of Regent Maximus's hooves. "You know what? I can get another one. Perhaps that one will continue to calm your Unicorn down."

Mr. Henshaw's voice was terse. "Thank you. Sorry about the mayhem. Maybe I can find you a replacement scarf before the Trident is over."

The prince touched his neck as if it missed the scarf. "That is very kind of you, but I doubt that would be possible. My country is a very tiny one, and I believe you would be hard-pressed to find the flag outside of its borders. I would, however, like to talk to you about . . . oh, but perhaps I should not keep your Unicorn standing out here like this. He has had a very trying day, I'm sure."

"We can take him to his stall, Mr. Henshaw," I offered, eager to escape the conversation. Mr. Henshaw was still upset, even if the prince didn't seem to be, and his annoyance at the situation was making me feel more anxious than I had even during the Unicorn chase itself.

"Are you sure?" Mr. Henshaw asked. "I really don't know . . ."

"Yes," I said with more certainty than I felt. "We'll be fine now that he's blindfolded."

"Just come looking for us if you hear screams," Tomas said in a hollow voice.

"I'll catch up in a moment," Mr. Henshaw said. He seemed relieved to have Regent Maximus taken out of his hands.

The walk back to the stalls was uneventful anyway. I hadn't yet learned how to make Regent Maximus ignore all the sights and sounds around him, but for the moment, it worked pretty well to just remove his ability to see or hear them. I kept up a steady stream of chatter to Regent Maximus to drown out the sounds of the building, and Tomas walked in front of us with his arms spread wide to clear all of the people from the aisle in front of us. A few of the other animal handlers recognized us as we headed back to the Unicorn section. Tomas held a finger to his lips to ask for quiet, and they made silent fist pumps of victory or made "okay" signs.

It should have felt nice, this silent recognition, but instead, I found that I was getting angrier at Regent Maximus. We had come further than this! Tomas and I had done so much for him! I kept seeing that image of him lunging out of the trailer toward me.

I got madder.

Finally, we came to Regent Maximus's assigned stall at the very end of the Unicorn section. I waited until Tomas had securely closed the door behind us to remove the prince's scarf from Regent Maximus's eyes. Immediately, the Unicorn staggered forward to press his face to the bars of the stall. He stared all around the Unicorn area.

I crossed my arms, glaring at him, waiting for him to turn back to me. He finally did, bits of straw from the Llamador ring matted in his forelock.

He caught my expression.

"Ahhh! Angry eyes—" he squealed.

"No!" I cut him off. "No more yelling! No running! No hiding! Regent Maximus, you could've hurt somebody. You could've hurt *me* or *Tomas*!"

"I would've been fine," Tomas interrupted. "I have my brother's football pads on underneath my shirt."

"That doesn't matter!" I said. I didn't want to be mean to Regent Maximus, but I held on to the image of him barreling toward me to keep my voice sounding stern. "We worked on this, Regent Maximus! We would never hurt you on purpose! You're *much bigger* than both of us!"

"I'm *so sorry,* Pip," Regent Maximus said in a sort of whisper. He sank down so low that I wasn't sure how he was doing it. It was like he had no bones in his legs.

I took a deep breath. "I know you're scared. But maybe next time be scared in one place instead of running all over the arena."

"I can be scared in one place," Regent Maximus said, nodding so hard he cracked his horn on the stall door and scurried away in surprise. "How about here?" he called from the corner of the stall.

"This is a safe place, not a place to be scared," I said. "It's supposed to be where you come to relax." I translated what he'd said for Tomas, because Tomas could hear only snorts and tiny whinnies.

Tomas considered. "What if we made it more like his stall at Mr. Henshaw's? Does he have anything there that makes him feel safe? Like a Noogie?"

"A what?" I asked.

Tomas blushed. "A Noogie? It's my blanket—never mind—"

"Oh!" I said. "I have something like that too! A stuffed Bog Wallow!"

Tomas looked relieved. I would've never made fun of him for his Noogie, but I bet his older brothers had. I put my hand on Regent Maximus's sticky shoulder. "Would you like us to get you a stuffed animal? Or a blanket?"

"Unicorns can *die* by ingesting blankets," Regent Maximus said fearfully.

"What *would* make you feel less afraid in here? Maybe some music?"

Regent Maximus sucked on his lips for a moment. "Maybe? Except not the sort with a lot of notes. Or the loud sort. Or the sort with singing."

That was how we wound up hunting down an old radio and tuning it to a station called Classical Chill. Both Tomas and Regent Maximus were pleased. And it was kind of a fun task, figuring out how to make the stall feel safer. While I drew a picture of me and Tomas and Regent Maximus together to hang on the wall, Tomas fastened a rolled blanket to the edge of the water bucket so that Regent Maximus wouldn't bump his head on the hard plastic. As I taped up the picture and put the radio out of Regent Maximus's reach, Tomas did a top-to-bottom safety inspection of the stall to put Regent Maximus's worries to rest. He made a long list of safety hazards, then started pulling supplies out of his first-aid kit.

"Tell him I'm going to start by taping down all the splinters," Tomas said.

I relayed the Tomas's words to Regent Maximus, then pointed to my drawing of him. "Look, Regent Maximus!"

I'd drawn Regent Maximus bigger and braver and prouder than he really was. It seemed like it'd be good for the Unicorn's self-confidence.

Regent Maximus pressed his face as close to the drawing as he could get while still being able to see it. I could see the whites all around his eyes and for a moment I thought that I'd somehow drawn something that pushed him over into terror.

But then he stamped his foot in a delighted way and said, "Oh! Good, yes. Good."

I began to scrub the Slurpee off his chest with a rag as Tomas went around and around us, laying big stripes of gauze all over the wall. "Is there anything else, Regent Maximus?"

"Can you stay here with me?" Regent Maximus asked.

"I don't think Aunt Emma would let me sleep in a stall," I said, which might not have been true. Aunt Emma herself slept in the stalls sometimes, like when a mother Griffin was about to have a litter, or that time an old Pegasus needed medicine every hour on the dot. It just didn't seem like a very good idea, to get Regent Maximus

used to me staying with him. What would he do on the nights when I couldn't?

"How about instead, I leave my jacket here with you. It'll smell like me," I suggested.

"All done here, Pip!" Tomas said. "Unless you think we can get an air purifier?"

"I don't think that'll be as easy to find as a spare radio," I said. I admired our handiwork. I wished that there was a section in Jeffrey Higgleston's guide about this—surely Regent Maximus couldn't be the only terrified Unicorn in existence. It would've been nice to have a little guidance. I made a note to begin keeping track of everything that helped Regent Maximus; I'd add it to my guide at the end of the show. Assuming we made it that far.

"Pip? Is that you?" a voice asked.

I frowned up at the rafters, expecting to see a Nectarbird or a Fancy Winged Squirrel.

Tomas caught my gaze. "Nope. I understood that too. It's a human."

"It is you!"

This time it was clear that the voice was coming from right outside the stall: a girl my age, with tidy red hair pulled into a bun. Unlike me, she had no ink smudges on her fingers or grime on her cheeks or hay stuck in her hair.

She wore a neat white shirt with an embroidered logo that read EVERSUN UNICORN FARMS, and had little Unicorn-shaped earrings in her ears.

"Oh," I said.

Because I knew this girl. And she knew me. Marisol Barrera was in my class back home in Atlanta, which meant she had been there for the Unicorn Incident—the stampede I'd caused at my school. And more important, her parents owned EverSun Unicorns. So not only had she been there for the Unicorn Incident . . . but it had been *her family's Unicorns* in the stampede.

I thought I'd been able to avoid Unicorn trouble—but Unicorn trouble had found me again!

CHAPTER 6

Shiny Things and Shiny People

I was so filled with worry at the sight of Marisol that I couldn't think of what to say. I just stood there making my fingers into fists and then stretching them out straight and then making them back into fists again. I knew I was fidgeting, but I couldn't make myself stop. How could I? I hadn't talked to her since the Unicorn stampede, and I knew she was going to say something terrible to me about it. And I would deserve it.

Marisol opened her mouth.

I waited for her to shout.

But instead she said, sunnily, "I *knew* it was you! I knew you were in Cloverton this summer, but I didn't know you'd be here!"

I hadn't expected her to smile, but she was smiling. She waved at Regent Maximus, who looked at her in a confused, slightly horrified way.

Tomas, meanwhile, nudged me with his shoulder and

gave me a meaningful look. When I didn't do anything, he nudged me even harder. This meant *Say something, Pip.*

I finally found my voice. "What—oh! Right. Marisol, this is my friend Tomas. He lives really close to my aunt's clinic."

Marisol nodded enthusiastically. "My parents told me about your aunt! She's a vet for magical creatures, right? That must be fun."

I squirmed a little inside, imagining being the topic of conversation in the Barrera household. I opened my mouth, but all that came out was "Er."

Marisol bounced a little closer to the stall—she sort of moved like an excited Unicorn, now that I thought about it, which was not at all how she walked back at school. She hooked her hands on the bars of the stall, face delighted, even though Regent Maximus still looked pretty disordered. "Is this your Unicorn? Or is he yours, Tomas?"

"I can't have pets," Tomas said. "I have allergies." As if to demonstrate his point, a very small turquoise bubble floated out of his right nostril. He'd taken some allergy pills, so it wasn't as dramatic as his earlier bubbles, but it was still a little awkward. We all three—four, really, because Regent Maximus watched it too—stared as it floated upward and popped on the ceiling.

I explained, "Neither. We're just helping out. Regent Maximus gets a little nervous."

Marisol stretched her hand through the bars toward Regent Maximus, as if he might possibly come over for a pet. He stared at her hand as if it were a viper. She didn't seem upset that he didn't want to approach, though. She said, "Lots of Unicorns get nervous before shows. Have you thought about adding some honeysuckle to his bedding? It might help calm him down even more."

"I'd never read about that," I said. "Does it really work?"

"Oh, yeah, loads! My parents figured it out by accident a couple of years ago!"

"That's cool. I'll see if we—"

But before I could finish my sentence, Marisol exclaimed, "EverSun has some you can use! I'll get it!"

She dashed down the aisle. I heard a bit of a scuffle, and then, just as Tomas and I exchanged a wide-eyed look, she reappeared, dragging a bale of honeysuckle.

"Open the door!" she exclaimed.

"I, uh—" I said. I opened the door, careful to be certain that Regent Maximus wasn't intending on galloping into the aisle, and Marisol shoved the bale inside.

Marisol began to pluck out big handfuls of

honeysuckle. "Just spread it around—it doesn't matter if it's messy!"

Together, we kicked the honeysuckle around the stall while Tomas lurked outside with a hand over his nose, just in case he turned out to be allergic to honeysuckle too.

At first, Regent Maximus flinched with every flying handful of honeysuckle. But then . . .

"Oh! I smell like joy! I smell like happiness!" Regent Maximus said dreamily as he rolled on his back. "The happiness is all over me! My skin is happiness!"

"He likes it," I said.

"I can tell!" Marisol said, laughing a little.

"Thanks," I said, surprised. "For letting us use EverSun's honeysuckle. You did that so fast. I didn't have time to say before."

She looked a little apologetic. "Sorry, Mom says I can be a little pushy. I just don't like to see Unicorns feeling terrible, if I can help it."

We all watched Regent Maximus roll around, grunting happily. He had honeysuckle stuck to the Slurpee left on his chest, making him look like he was growing mold, but he didn't seem to care. I couldn't remember the last time I'd seen him so relaxed. I definitely had a new fact to write into the *Guide to Magical Creatures* when I got home.

I took a deep breath, working up my nerve, and then I said, "I sort of thought you might still be mad at me."

Marisol blinked. "For what?"

I confessed, "Because of the, uh, Unicorn Incident back at school."

"Oh, no," Marisol said. "I knew you weren't trying to hurt anybody. You just love animals and got carried away. I . . . I love them too, especially Unicorns. And my mom says I get carried away all the time!"

We smiled cautiously at each other. Maybe Marisol and I had more in common than I thought. I asked, "Do you want to look around with Tomas and me? We were going to go see the Manticores."

"Oh . . . I can't," Marisol said.

My heart dipped. I'd gone too far. Just because she wanted to help Regent Maximus and wasn't angry at me for the stampede didn't mean that she wanted to hang out with me. But then she said, "I was just headed back to the wash stalls because I promised to groom one of the EverSun Unicorns. Do you guys want to come with *me*?"

Tomas and I both regarded Regent Maximus. The Unicorn was now curled in the honeysuckle like a puppy, munching happily on honeycomb, gazing at the picture I'd drawn him as if it were his favorite television program. He looked pretty comfortable, even if his stall looked a little bit ridiculous, what with the pictures and gauze and the curtain we'd fashioned out of a saddle blanket and bag clips.

"Do you mind if we go?" I asked Regent Maximus. I said it in a casual way so that Marisol wouldn't think I was strange. "Mr. Henshaw should be coming by at any minute."

"I have happiness stuck to the top of my mouth," Regent Maximus replied through the honeycomb.

That seemed to mean that he would be fine—at least for now.

We let Marisol lead us down the aisle to the general large-animal section. She chattered enthusiastically as she walked, twice as loud as Tomas and I put together.

". . . I'm supposed to make sure Duchess is really in good shape, all groomed up, clean as she can be. We think she might place this year! First, second, or third. There's a stallion named Forever Sunshine that we think will get first, and a purple Unicorn we think will get second, but even third place at the Trident is a big deal. And we've been working with her for *ages,* she's so steady. Look, there she is in the cross ties, all the way down there!"

We'd entered a section of wash stalls, full of all sorts of large magical animals. Each concrete floor had a drain in the middle, and there were metal rings placed at various places along the wall to attach lead ropes to. Some of the stalls were empty, their floors still wet and sudsy, but most had some kind of creature in them.

In the stall closest to us was a Two-Headed Greater Nackerbaum, both heads securely tied. A woman was spraying it down with a hose nozzle, and every time the water hit the Nackerbaum's skin, the liquid hissed and immediately evaporated. I knew from *Jeffrey Higgleston's Guide to Magical Creatures* that this was because of the Nackerbaum's high internal temperature. What I didn't know from the *Guide* was how loud the Nackerbaum could be. Every time the water splashed over it, both heads shook wildly, and it shrieked, "*WATER!*" It was hard to tell if the Nackerbaum was happy or sad about it.

In the next stall was a squat Bricksnout. Its skin had turned completely solid, and the man washing it was using a pumice stone instead of a brush to wash it. The sound was like fingernails on a chalkboard. Tomas winced.

In the stall after that was a pair of animals that I didn't immediately recognize; they looked completely unfamiliar soaking wet. I realized after a moment that they had to be Llamadors, both beautifully tricolored, with long eyelashes. Their handler kept slapping their muzzles gently because they wouldn't stop guzzling soapy water and then coughing up suds. It was amazing how different they looked with their fur soaked to their skin.

Really, the *Guide* should have pictures of some magical creatures both wet and dry—because all of these creatures looked like entirely different species when soaked.

Duchess, Marisol's Unicorn charge, was in the second to last stall, standing patiently in cross ties—one lead attached to each side of her halter so that she couldn't turn around inside the stall. She had just enough free space to curl her neck prettily and look into a bucket of water at her reflection. She was talking to it.

"Hello, my name is Duchess. *Hello*, my name is *Duch*ess. Hello! My name! Is DUCHESS!"

"Stop it," said a voice from the final stall. I glanced in: The voice was coming from a beautiful golden Standard Griffin. The Griffin stood perfectly still with his eyes closed as his handler ran water between the Griffin's feathered ears. He barely opened his beak to complain, "No more."

"I'm so beautiful," Duchess told the bucket.

"Oh, please," said the Griffin, voice dry and grim.

"You're number one," Duchess added.

"Make her stop," said the Griffin.

"Look at those eyes!" Duchess continued to her reflection.

"I beg you," the Griffin pleaded.

"Duchess, Duchess, Duchess," Duchess said.

"Unicorns are the worst," the Griffin muttered.

"This is Duchess," Marisol told me and Tomas.

So I heard, I thought. I was a little annoyed to see that Duchess was as beautiful as she'd been telling herself. She was a pale purple color, like the underside of a cloud at sunset, except for her knees, muzzle, and mane, which were all silvered. Her face was delicately dished and her eyes were large and lustrous.

Marisol regarded the Unicorn proudly. "She's not as uniquely colored as your Regent Maximus, of course, but she has really good lines and does well in the agility contest."

"She's beautiful. What does she have to do to win the Trident? Trot around the ring like the other creatures we saw?"

"Oh, no! The Trident is much more involved. There are three rounds. Round one is just a simple trot around the ring. Round two is an agility course. And round three is the princess round. They add all the scores up to find a winner. Here—" She reached into the back pocket of her jeans and showed me a Triple Trident Unicorn Show bulletin. It'd clearly been folded and refolded a bunch of times.

I studied the bulletin, then handed it back. "So what happens if Duchess wins? Is there another contest after the Trident?" I asked.

Marisol shrugged. "Oh, sure, every state has one, though the Trident is especially prestigious. If she doesn't do well, we'll probably sell her, since she's getting a little old."

"Sell her!" Tomas said in a shocked voice. I was glad he was as surprised as I was. I was also glad Duchess couldn't understand what Marisol was saying.

Marisol stepped back, alarmed at his tone. "Oh—um. That's sort of how it works. You can't keep *every* Unicorn, so you only hang on to your top winners. Another stable without as many well-bred Unicorns would love to have one like Duchess!"

"But don't you . . . don't you care about her?" I asked.

Now Marisol looked hurt. "Of course! But that's how the show world runs—there's not enough room to keep every Unicorn forever. Besides, we wouldn't just sell her to anyone. She'd go to a wonderful stable. And she'd be the most beautiful Unicorn there—I think she'd like that."

At that moment, Duchess was singing a little song. "From the tip of my horn to the end of my tail, compared to me, all the others are snails!"

She really would like being the most beautiful in a stable. Still, it seemed a little strange. I guess I was used to thinking of magical creatures as part of the family, not something you could just get rid of if you didn't have room. I didn't think Regent Maximus would care about being the most beautiful in a stable. I think he cared more about who else was in the stable with him.

Marisol tapped on a blue wooden star on Duchess's stall door, right beneath the plaque with her longer, fancier show name written on it. "See this? A few people have talked to my parents about her already, but we're going to wait and see how she does."

Tomas's expression had clouded over. "The star means she's for sale?"

Marisol nodded.

"For all Unicorns, that's what the star means? That they're for sale?" Tomas asked again.

Marisol looked a little confused, but then she nodded again, a bit slower this time—like Tomas might not be understanding her.

"All Unicorns with a star—" Tomas went on.

I jumped in, "Are for sale, Tomas. What's up?"

Without another word, he jogged back down the Unicorn aisle. I bolted after him, only catching up as he skidded to a stop in front of Regent Maximus's stall.

He pointed.

Right beside Regent Maximus's name was a blue wooden star.

CHAPTER 7

The Little Country with a Big Problem

"But he can't just *sell* Regent Maximus!" I said the next morning.

We were all in the car headed back to the next day of the show; it was another sunny, muggy day. Callie, looking fresh-faced once more, sat in the passenger seat, savoring the air-conditioning while it lasted. In the back-seat next to me, Tomas dug through his backpack of emergency supplies.

"Pip, just because he's *available* for sale doesn't mean he'll be sold. And besides, Regent Maximus isn't exactly . . . um . . . well, let's just say I don't think there will be lots of potential buyers." Aunt Emma paused to shout at a passing driver—Aunt Emma's normally unflappable exterior vanished only when confronted with other drivers—and then, in a calmer voice, she added, "Anyway, Mr. Henshaw spent a lot of money on Regent Maximus, hoping for a Unicorn he could have fun with at shows. That hasn't quite worked out. If Regent Maximus doesn't win, Mr. Henshaw will have to get back his money somehow—and selling Regent Maximus, even at a lower price, will help. I don't want you to be upset if Mr. Henshaw *does* decide to sell Regent Maximus to a home that will better appreciate Regent Maximus's . . . personality!"

Tomas and I exchanged a resentful look.

"How about we stop for some sweet tea on the way?" Aunt Emma pulled into a little, faded service station. "Let's not let this ruin your day."

"I want soda," Callie replied.

"I'm fine with water," Tomas said. "I don't want to get high blood sugar."

"I do," said Callie.

Aunt Emma opened the car door, letting in a wave of heat. "Okay, so soda for Callie, water for Tomas, tea for me and Pip. Oh, hey, Pip, while you're waiting, you and Tomas should look at your map and find the Glimmerbeast area. Don't forget you promised to see if Mariah wanted any help with her Rockshines."

I had totally forgotten. It was a little annoying to think I had to do that when Regent Maximus clearly needed our help, but I guessed I *had* said I'd come find her.

Aunt Emma headed into the service station. As soon as she had gone, Callie twisted in her seat. "Is it true? Did you really meet *the* Prince Temujin? And *steal his scarf*? Do you even know who he is?"

"One of the Unicorn judges?" I replied.

"OTHER THAN THAT?"

"A prince?" Tomas offered.

"OTHER THAN *THAT*?"

We blinked at her.

"Of course you two little raccoons have no idea," she said. "His mother is *the* Diana Kiley. Don't just stare at me! You have to know who *she* is?"

We blinked at her.

"Ugh, well, Diana Kiley is basically my hero. She originated the starring roles in all my favorite Broadway shows. I *have* to meet Prince Temujin— if he likes me, maybe he'll introduce me to Diana! Or at least pass on my headshot. Some people say I look like a younger version of her, you know." She pulled her hair over her shoulder and pursed her lips. "Connections are very important when you're going to be an actress."

"What is he the prince of?" Tomas asked. I was glad he asked, because I wanted to know too.

"Galatolia," Callie said. "It's near Turkey or something. I think. It's not very big, and I don't think it has a lot of money—"

"Galatolia!" I exclaimed. "The five largest endangered

GALATOLIA:
The Little Country with the Big Problem

Galatolia is at once blessed with a number of unique species and cursed with a population unable to preserve them. A variety of factors have led to the decline of three of their endangered species.

Chicken farmers seeking to protect their hens have hunted the egg-loving Snoozle nearly to extinction.

The Paradise Frog suffers from a love of street lights. Attracted to the artificial glow, the Frogs fly up to the lights and remain forever, never leaving to lay eggs.

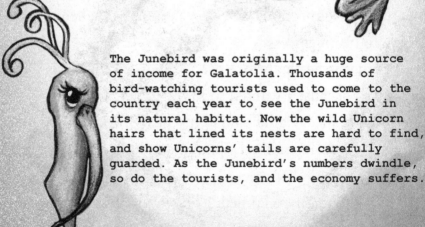

The Junebird was originally a huge source of income for Galatolia. Thousands of bird-watching tourists used to come to the country each year to see the Junebird in its natural habitat. Now the wild Unicorn hairs that lined its nests are hard to find, and show Unicorns' tails are carefully guarded. As the Junebird's numbers dwindle, so do the tourists, and the economy suffers.

magical creatures are from Galatolia! Jeffrey Higgleston calls it 'the Little Country with a Big Problem'!"

Callie rolled her eyes. "Of *course* that's what you know. Just don't cause a *scene* today, all right? Don't steal his scarf or his car or whatever. I don't want him to remember me for *that*."

We hadn't really been the ones to cause the scene yesterday, but there was no point telling Callie that. Also, today was the first round of competition for Regent Maximus, which meant there was a good chance that he might cause yet another scene, but there was also no point in telling Callie *that* either.

As she swiveled back around in her seat, I turned to Tomas and said urgently, "Tomas, we *have* to make sure Regent Maximus does a good job at the Trident."

Tomas didn't say anything out loud, but his expression said clearly that he was remembering saving me from a trampling Unicorn only the day before.

"I'm not saying he has to *win* the entire show! But there's no way Mr. Henshaw will want to keep him if Regent Maximus just shakes and hides and quivers around the ring. We've helped Regent Maximus be brave before. Maybe we can train him up to be a real show Unicorn!"

"Are you talking about a different Regent Maximus?" Tomas asked.

"Tomas!"

"Okay, okay." Tomas held up his hands. "But I don't know the first thing about training Unicorns. Do you?"

"Nope," I said, digging into my backpack. "But Jeffery Higgleston does! There's an entire section in the *Guide*." I flipped through it hurriedly. Buried deep in the fat *Guide* section on Unicorns were a few pages on training.

"Here!" I said triumphantly, opening the book in my lap to show him.

Tomas leaned toward me to look at the *Guide*. "I'm not really sure Regent Maximus *is* meant to mince."

"Sure he is! He's a show Unicorn!" I said, but as I flipped through the pages, I had to admit that these tips didn't seem like the sort that would help a Unicorn like Regent Maximus. He was probably afraid of glitter, for starters, so I didn't see how tossing it at his hooves would accomplish anything but him fleeing in terror. Without much conviction, I added, "Anyway, all he has to do in this round is make it through one lap around the ring."

Aunt Emma opened the door, her arms full of drinks. "I'm back! You guys ready?"

"There is no getting ready for this," Tomas replied darkly.

It wasn't like he was *wrong*.

We went to Regent Maximus's stall right away, and when I explained to him that we were going to help him do a lap with confidence, he seemed on board. He even did a cheerful spin, being careful not to touch the walls. Once he found out, however, that the show lap had to take place *outside* of his stall, his good mood vanished.

"*What?!*" Regent Maximus cried. "*Outside?*"

"It's nearly as easy as walking a circle in your stall!" I insisted.

"Noooooooooooooooooo." His whinny echoed down the hall as Tomas came back with a few bottles of water.

"I'm guessing this isn't going very well?" Tomas asked. "Here, have some water. Hydration is important."

I accepted a bottle of water, even though I didn't think hydration would help my *current* problem. "Would you read what the *Guide* says about this again? It's just out there."

I had propped the *Guide to Magical Creatures* on two lavender bales outside the stall. Tomas leaned down to read it out loud. The first section was on training a Unicorn to walk on a lead in the "show style," which was a sort of high-step prancy walk.

In a cheery voice, I said, "Did you hear that, Regent Maximus? If you do a lap around the show ring, we'll get you some fresh honeycomb!"

Regent Maximus sank down low into his lavender bedding and wailed, "How will I be able to eat it? I'll surely be dead by then."

"No, you'll be fine," I continued soothingly. "Just imagine that honeycomb. Dripping with honey. Oozing with honey."

He managed to shiver with worry and drool with anticipation at the same time. "Can I get the honeycomb now? It'll be a good last meal. If I don't choke on it."

"Only after."

Regent Maximus laid his head on the bedding and closed his eyes.

"I don't think honeycomb or candied apples are going to do it," I told Tomas. "What else does it say?"

"Nothing. Do you think there's something he wants *more* than honeycomb or candied apples?"

"Is there something you'd like more than honeycomb or apples?" I asked the Unicorn, but he didn't lift his head. He looked as if he had been dropped from a very great height and now was embedded in the lavender.

Both Tomas and I turned our attention to Callie, who was approaching. She'd put on so much shiny lip gloss that her mouth sort of looked like a piece of watermelon.

"Hey, Pip-squeak," Callie said, "Oh, and you too, Tomas, I guess. Mom says you're late. You're supposed to be over in the Shinyrock or Rockyshines or whatever-they're-called's pen helping Ms. Gould, remember?"

"I remember," I said. "We just wanted to try to work with Regent Maximus a little beforehand."

Callie eyed the Unicorn, who had not moved except to open his eyes. "It looks like it's going really great."

"He's thinking," I said. "Regent Maximus, we'll be back, okay?"

"Doom," Regent Maximus whispered into the bedding. "Doom doom doom."

Tomas opened and closed the stall door for me as I left the Unicorn behind, still murmuring "Doom" into the ground. I didn't want Callie to talk anymore about how the training was going—or rather, not going—so I asked quickly, "Have you, uh, seen the prince?"

Callie brightened. "No. But I *have* nearly learned how to sing the Galatolia national anthem! I need to keep practicing the high E over C part. Want to hear?"

I had heard a lot of Callie's singing since I had come to stay in Cloverton. And it wasn't that she was bad. It was just . . . a lot of singing.

"Rockshines," Tomas said, as either a reminder or a rescue.

"Yeah, we gotta go!" I said. "I'll hear it later!"

As we sprinted off, I heard the Unicorns groan in near unison as Callie launched into the Galatolia national anthem anyhow.

"Doom," sang Regent Maximus, in the same key as Callie. He hit the high E over C perfectly. "Doom!"

CHAPTER 8

Heeeeeeeeyyyyyyyyyyyyyy, Part Two

When Tomas and I arrived at the Glimmerbeast area, it appeared as if half the pens were empty. After that day with Ms. Gould at the clinic, I knew better, though. The pens were full of invisible Glimmerbeasts.

It was a very odd sight. Some pens were full of floating collars. Some were full of floating harnesses. The strangest was a pen that was labeled Zundersnouts. They must have been tagged, because dark, ghostly numbers hung in the air.

I tried to get excited about helping out with the Rockshines—as excited as I'd felt that first day—but I kept thinking about Regent Maximus whispering, "*Doom*," and Mr. Henshaw selling him. In comparison, the Rockshines seemed incredibly unimportant.

"What do Rockshines look like when they're visible?" Tomas asked, with a wary glance at a pen that contained an equal number of visible and invisible Shadyhogs.

Glimmerbeasts

Glimmerbeasts are a large class of
magical creatures, with populations
on every single continent and species
of every size, but they all have two
things in common: All Glimmerbeasts
have hooves, and all Glimmerbeasts
have the ability to become invisible
when stressed. Here are three of the
rarest Glimmerbeasts:

Crested
Curly
Woo

BadgerSnick

HabberFrabber

I didn't want to tell him the truth, which was: They looked *boring*. Like slow, unmagical sheep. The invisible part was interesting, but otherwise, they were big, clumsy, and unclever. They didn't seem to have anything interesting to say. All they wanted to do was eat and be left alone. Anything that got in the way of that made them go invisible.

"They're, uh, brown," I said. "Ish. Brownish. And . . . round? Roundish."

"Over there?" Tomas pointed. Sure enough, I could see some brownish forms, and as we got closer, I could hear: "*Heeeyyyy! Heeey. HEEEEEEEY? Heeeey.*"

"Pip! It's Pip, right?" Mariah Gould's voice carried over the sounds of the Rockshine's shouts. "I'm glad you made it!"

Now that we were close to the Rockshines, Tomas was staring at them. The entire herd was visible as far as I could tell, standing up to their knees in ordinary hay, chewing slowly and occasionally saying, "*Heeeeey.*" They came in brown and gray and brownish gray and grayish brown. A few of them had clearly been groomed for the show ring, which just meant they had a little less drool on their chins. The hay had completely captured their attention, and they didn't look up as we talked.

Tomas stared at them. They stared at the hay.

"Sorry it took me so long to get over here!" I told Ms. Gould.

"I heard you were busy wrangling Unicorns!" Ms. Gould said, laughing at her own joke. "I'm so glad that you've come by to help, because I've got to run this paperwork over to the show office and the Rockshines need their eyes wiped down."

The Rockshines blinked at Ms. Gould with gummy, bored eyes.

A building full of incredible animals and a stall full of a terrified Unicorn that needed me, and this was where I was. I wrinkled my nose.

Ms. Gould misunderstood my expression. "It's not a hard job as long as you aren't afraid of them. Oh, is this another helper too?"

Tomas peered up at her. "Do they bite?"

"Oh, no," she said. "They're very calm animals! Pip saw Bucky over there"—she paused to point at a Rockshine that looked like all of the other Rockshines—"at his worst, but that was because he was in an unfamiliar location away from the herd. All together like this? They are fairly unflappable."

"Do they have *fur* or *hair*?" Tomas asked with a shrewd expression.

"I'm sorry?"

"Hair is hypoallergenic, usually," Tomas said.

Ms. Gould looked glad to be asked. "Oh! Well, yes, their hide is more like hair. They're a great livestock choice for people with allergies, because they don't produce any irritating dander or—look at the time! I really better go run this to the office. Here are the rags to clean their eyes. If you run into any problems, just talk to Deedra over there with the Shadyhogs. She'll help you out. Thanks again."

After she had gone, I sighed. Even the Shadyhogs looked more interesting than the Rockshines . . . and they were all talking about varieties of dirt.

"It's when it has bits of gravel in it," said one. "That's what I am talking about."

"Gravel? No, I was talking about silt. When it's just a little gritty between your teeth."

"What about a good loam? Some fluffy muck is where it is at."

"None of you have said anything about clay."

I couldn't tell if they were talking about lying in it or eating it.

Anything but Rockshines.

Reluctantly, I said, "You don't have to help with this, Tomas, if you don't want to. I was the one who agreed to help, after all."

Shadyhog

Thick snout can break roots, shift rocks, and crack refrigerator doors

When visible, Shadyhogs are often patterned with multicolor spots for further camouflage in dappled light

Cloven hooves must be trimmed using diamond-tipped shears

Shadyhogs are covered with short, scratchy hairs that are uncomfortable to the touch; they are shaved for the show ring

---

SIZE: 38-48" at shoulder
WEIGHT: 300-500 lbs.
DESCRIPTION: One of the largest varieties of Glimmerbeast, Shadyhogs were both loved and feared in medieval Europe. A wild Shadyhog could cause serious injury if disturbed, but the domesticated Shadyhog still has no equal in the quest for delicate wild truffles. In France, Shadyhogs are still used today for rooting out rare mushrooms.

Tomas didn't reply, so I turned. And then turned again. "Tomas?"

He was nowhere to be found. There were fewer people here than there had been when we first arrived in this area, but I still couldn't see him among them.

Then I caught sight of his bright blue backpack. He had let himself in among the Rockshines already and was, in fact, *hugging* one of them.

I climbed over the temporary metal fence to join him. Tomas still had his arms wrapped around a Rockshine's neck. His cheek was pressed up against its brown-gray or gray-brown cheek. The Rockshine looked bland. Tomas looked *happy*.

"Tomas?" I asked. "What are you doing?"

Tomas didn't let go. "These are the *best* animals."

He didn't normally make jokes, but I narrowed my eyes. "Are you being funny?"

Releasing the creature, Tomas looked at its face. It sort of looked at his face, and also sort of at the ceiling, as its eyes were pointed two different directions. "These are my favorite. *Look at them!*"

I *was* looking at them.

Tomas hugged the Rockshine again. "They are the best. Look! He isn't going to bite or gore or suffocate me! He's just happy to be here! And I'm happy *for* him!" he said, tugging it even closer. The Rockshine strained to get back to its hay.

I couldn't decide which was more shocking: that anyone found the Rockshine to be *the best*, or that Tomas Ramirez was *hugging a magical creature*.

"Well . . . I'm . . . glad you like them," I told him.

"What are they saying, Pip? Are they saying nice things? I bet they are."

The Rockshines, in true Rockshine fashion, were mostly just saying "Hey" to one another, and to the hay, and to me, and to Tomas, and to their feet. I told Tomas this.

"Oh! Yes, here—have some hay!" Tomas said, unconcerned by just how little these animals had to say. Grabbing a handful of hay, he offered it to the nearest Rockshine, looking delighted when it mouthed it right out of his palm.

I held out one of the rags. "Do you want to wipe its face?"

Tomas tenderly dabbed its face. ("Look! It doesn't mind at all!") As he did, I noticed that the crowd around us was thinning. It felt, actually, like we were the only humans still left in this part of the arena. It took me a moment to figure it out—everyone must be headed to the center ring for round one of the Unicorn show!

Grabbing a rag of my own, I moved quickly through

the herd, wiping their eyes with a lot less affection than Tomas. Sometimes I moved too fast and I saw one begin to go invisible. I forced myself to move more deliberately; if the herd went invisible, we'd never be able to finish our task. And it wasn't Ms. Gould's fault that I wanted to be elsewhere. A promise was a promise.

Which was hard to remember when somewhere, Regent Maximus was getting ready to go into the ring for the first time. I should be there.

I had finished wiping down about twenty animals when I shot a glance back over to Tomas. He was still working carefully at wiping the stains off the first animal's face. He kept pausing to pat it gently between its ears.

I jumped as the Rockshine closest to me said, "*Heyyy.*" Its neighbor also said, "*Heeeeyyyyy,*" without lifting its head. The rest of the herd joined in: "*Heyyy! Heeey. Heeyyyyyy.*" Then Ms. Gould's voice said, "I'm back! As you can hear—they know their mother, don't they? Oh! You've done such a good job! Can I repay the favor?"

The overhead loudspeaker announced, "Attention, Trident Guests: All Unicorns, please report to the main ring for round one of the Triple Trident."

"Tomas, that's Regent Maximus!" I exclaimed so loudly that the three Rockshines nearest me immediately vanished. "I'm sorry, Ms. Gould, but we've got to go!"

CHAPTER
— 9 —

A Spiral of Doom

We sprinted through the mostly empty corridors of the competition. It was impossible to even *see* the center ring, though, because the crowd of people around it had grown so thick. Tomas and I jumped up and down, trying to get a good view over all the grown-ups' shoulders. No use.

"Come on!" I said. I grabbed the strap of Tomas's backpack to guide him through the crowd, ducking under people's arms and swerving around baby carriages.

Were we too late? Had it already started?

We finally broke through to the front of the crowd. The Unicorns were only just starting to enter the ring from a gate over to the right. The announcer called out the first Unicorn's name from a platform at the opposite end of the ring as Tomas and I jogged along the edge of the fence. The loudspeaker echoed all around, like a voice underwater. All I could think was how overwhelming this must seem to Regent Maximus.

"Do you see him?" Tomas called up to me.

"Not yet!" I called back. What if Mr. Henshaw hadn't even been able to get Regent Maximus out of his stall? *Faster, run faster!*

Reaching the end of the fence, we peered over it, trying to see down the line of Unicorns waiting to enter the ring. Tomas's hair was all standing up again, but he didn't bother to pat it down. Instead, he pointed. "There he is!"

Regent Maximus stood at the very back of the line, just behind a very pale peach Unicorn with a tangerine-colored mane. Even from here, I could see his knees knocking in fright.

"Regent Maximus!" I shouted.

"Pip!" Mr. Henshaw said.

"PIP!" Regent Maximus wailed.

Thunderous applause welcomed the next Unicorn in line. The other waiting Unicorns all thrilled at the sound of adoration. With their perfectly coiffed tails and their coats curried until the building lights winked off them, they all looked just like the *Guide*'s illustrations of trained Unicorns.

Regent Maximus, on the other hand, looked . . . well. At least he was clean. Mr. Henshaw had managed to finish getting most of the red Slurpee off his chest. His tail wasn't brushed, but Mr. Henshaw seemed to have picked most of the straw out of it.

But unlike the other Unicorns, Regent Maximus's horn was pointed at the ground. He was so folded in on himself that he seemed half the size of the other Unicorns.

I climbed the first board of the fence to get closer and asked Mr. Henshaw, "How is he doing?"

"You can see him. Not grand," Mr. Henshaw replied grimly. "Too bad he can't be blindfolded. Come on, buddy, just one lap around the ring."

"Just one lap," I repeated encouragingly so that Regent Maximus could understand.

"A spiral of doom," Regent Maximus sniffled. "*Doooooooooom.*"

Mr. Henshaw couldn't understand what his Unicorn was saying—it sounded only like a series of low-pitched whinnies—but he got the gist. He looked exasperated. "I'm not so sure he can manage the show-style walk. Or any walk at all."

In the ring, the Unicorn with the tangerine hair tossed his head back magnificently as he passed in front of the purple-cloth-covered table where Prince Temujin and the other judges sat. He chanted in time with his hooves hitting the ground: "I'm so pretty-pretty-pretty-pretty."

He seemed to be a crowd favorite—the people closest

to him went wild and the ring was an explosion of photography flashes. As he minced out of the ring, I had to admit, he was particularly beautiful. His tail was so orange and bright I nearly had to squint to look at it.

"Broken ankles, torn ACLs, hoof rot, twisted tibias," Regent Maximus said, tossing his head with each word. It took me a moment to realize he was listing off all the bad things that could happen to his legs.

"This is probably pointless," Mr. Henshaw said, as Regent Maximus nearly yanked the lead out of his hand when he said *tibias*. "The only way I got him over here was a blindfold; I should have known better."

Suddenly, an idea hit me. I remembered how we had blindfolded him with the scarf, and how I had wished that Regent Maximus could learn to ignore all of the sights and sounds of the show.

I clambered over the fence.

"Pip, what are you doing? We're going in next," Mr. Henshaw said. "Probably."

Taking Regent Maximus's cheeks in my hands, I guided his quivering face so that he was looking at me. "Look at me, Regent Maximus."

His eyes rolled over to the ring, then over to the crowd.

"Regent Maximus. Look. At. Me."

His eyes rolled to me.

"I'm not scary, right?" I asked.

"Mmmmrmmm mrmmmm," he said, which wasn't really an answer. But I felt him stop quivering a little.

"I want you to look just at me. No matter where you are in the ring, don't look at anything else. Only me. Nothing can hurt you as long as you're looking just at me. Don't look *anywhere else*."

He started to roll his eyes away but stopped himself. "Really?"

"Yes," I said. And it wasn't totally a lie, right? Nothing was going to hurt him in the ring either way. "Just keep your eyes on me. I'll be right here at the gate. Tomas and I will wave—right, Tomas?"

Tomas waved a little, like he wanted to show Regent Maximus he could do it. Mr. Henshaw looked dubious—probably he thought I was being silly by talking directly to his Unicorn. But even he could see that Regent Maximus had at least stopped shivering.

The announcer's voice split through the speakers. "Ladies and gentleman, that was Forever Sparkle Stables' Forever Sunshine! And now our final entry in the Triple Trident! Callaloo's Multicolored Lies the Head That Wears the Crown!"

CHAPTER 10

Walk, Trot, Slink

Regent Maximus entered the ring.

I thought people were probably expecting an especially grand Unicorn, given how fancy Regent Maximus's show name was. Probably they were expecting Jeffrey Higgleston's Ideal Unicorn. But instead of prancing like a crown-wearer, Regent Maximus crept out from the gate, lagging behind Mr. Henshaw. He didn't mince or toss his mane like the other Unicorns had; he crawled. Or at least, it was the closest thing to crawl that a Unicorn can do. Picture a lizard with really long legs—legs that, to his credit, he was lifting up as high as he could, in a sort of slinky version of the Unicorn show-style walk. He kept his glorious rainbow tail pulled tight between his legs, and his ears were so flat on his white head that he looked like he didn't have any.

The announcer's microphone squealed as the audience fell silent. The judges glanced at one another warily, like perhaps they were being recorded for a funny joke video.

To his credit, he didn't stop. He kept his head arced around, so he could watch me as he slunk-pranced around the first half of the ring. But he didn't stop.

"Pip! I'm doing it! My ankles feel fine!" he squealed as he rounded the far side, near the judges. He rose a tiny bit, picking up his feet even higher, like he was gingerly stepping over invisible spiders.

"You're doing great!" I called to him. The crowd was so quiet that everyone turned to look at me. I wanted so badly to step back and disappear, but there was no way Regent Maximus would finish his lap if I wasn't there. So, the same way he was focusing on *me*, I focused on him.

"Come on, Regent Maximus!" Tomas yelled, much to my surprise. He didn't like people looking at him any more than I did. "You can do it!"

And to my greater surprise, the crowd laughed a little. And to my greatest surprise, they started cheering Regent Maximus too.

"Come on, buddy!" a man near me said.

"Halfway there!" someone else said cheerily.

"Go, go, go!"

"Show 'em how it's done, Recent Masi—what was his name again?"

Regent Maximus couldn't understand them, of course, but he could tell they were cheering for him. He looked a little frightened by it, and for a moment, I thought he was going to break. I pointed to my eyeballs, and he focused on them. And this time, when the crowd cheered, he began to scurry a bit faster. A bit faster still. And a bit faster still, until he was *almost* walking beside Mr. Henshaw. Mr. Henshaw risked patting the Unicorn's neck in support.

The crowd cheered louder.

Regent Maximus still had his eyes firmly locked on me, but now he had his ears up enough that you could at least *see* them. He was listening to the crowd and not spooking! He was doing it!

I motioned him toward me enthusiastically, while Tomas clapped.

He made it to the gate. *He made it.* Hurrying over, I hugged him tightly—

"Careful, Pip! You'll collapse my windpipe!" he said worriedly. "Now can I go back to the stall and look at my picture again?"

"Absolutely," I told him.

Overhead, we heard the announcer's voice booming one last time: "Ladies and gentlemen, let's give one last round of applause for your thirteen Triple Trident contenders! On to round two!"

He'd made it through one round, anyway.

CHAPTER
— 11 —

Scandal! Scandal! Scandal!

I never thought there would come a time when I was happy to be done with a day of magical creature showing, but I was feeling pretty good being back at the clinic after a long day of Rockshines and Unicorns. My ears were still ringing with the remembered sounds of animal and people noises—it was no wonder Regent Maximus was overwhelmed.

Even Aunt Emma sounded tired as she walked into the house and sloughed off her bags by the door. "Pip, I hate to ask you to do *more* work, but do you think you could tend to the animals in the back cages while I work on a few of the patients that need my attention? Callie, can you order pizza?"

"I thought you'd never ask," Callie said.

"I don't mind," I replied. It would be nice to do something in the relative quiet. I loved Aunt Emma, and Tomas was my best friend, and even Callie was all right when she wasn't in a raging mood, but sometimes I just needed to have some absolute quiet or I started to feel a little strange.

So I really didn't mind cleaning out the cages in the back room. I went through all of the routines listed on the poster by the door.

I also went through *my* routine, which was to run over all the facts I knew about the animals in the cages and see if I could use them to make them any happier. For instance, I knew the Short-Winged Salamanders liked to stay warm, so when I let them out of their cage to clean it, I plugged in a heating pad for them to cluster on.

"Like summer!" one said, sounding pleased.

"Like fire!" said another.

"Like the sun!" said a third.

"I'm *burning*!" said a fourth.

"*YAY!*" they all said together.

I sprayed down their cage and left the cleaner for a moment to soak in. While I waited, I removed a folded-up show bulletin from my pocket, the same as the one Marisol had shown me. I'd picked one up on the way out the door.

Round two was "under saddle"—which meant Mr. Henshaw was going to have to *ride* Regent Maximus through the whole thing. I'd ridden Regent Maximus once before and had lived to tell the tale. But *I* could talk him through all the things that scared him. Mr. Henshaw didn't have that ability.

Still—between me, Tomas, and the *Guide*, surely we could train Regent Maximus up in time. We had to! Even if the round was too complicated for Regent Maximus to keep eye contact with us the entire time, he surely had to have gotten some confidence from surviving round one.

Just then, Callie flew through the hallway door. She made an *ew, gross* face when she saw the Short-Winged Salamanders all lumped together; the Salamanders made their own version of the same face when they saw her.

Callie purposefully looked away from them and told me, "Mom just got a call from the show authorities. Scandal, scandal, scandal, at the show!"

She didn't say anything else, and I realized that she was waiting for me to reply. I echoed, "Scandal?"

Callie folded her arms across her chest. "Yes! Someone waited until the show hours were over, and then snuck into the Unicorn barn area to cut off one of the Unicorn's tails."

My heart chugged in my chest. "Not Regent Maximus!"

"No, some Unicorn called Forever Shines the Sun or something like that— it was that pretty orange-haired one everyone liked in the first round. The tail was sawed right off—it's just this long now, apparently." She held her hands seven inches apart. "Scandal! Scandal!"

"But why? Sabotage?" I asked.

"Why else?" Callie asked. "It was one of the top Unicorns that got a haircut. Now all the others have a better chance of winning. *Maybe* your dear Mr. Henshaw did it, since there's no other way that his Unicorn will win."

I frowned and began to collect my cleaning supplies. "That doesn't seem like him."

Callie shrugged, aggressively unconvinced. She didn't like Mr. Henshaw because he'd asked Aunt Emma out on dates a few times. Aunt Emma had turned him down, of course—she was still hoping my uncle Grady would be found, even though he'd been missing ever since he went out on a mission seven years before to prove Dragons still existed.

I liked to think that I'd be unbiased when it came to Unicorn safety. But it just didn't seem like Mr. Henshaw to cut off a Unicorn tail to get ahead in competition.

"There are easier ways to win," I said. "Like not buying a Unicorn like Regent Maximus."

"Yeah, well, he's stuck with him now, isn't he?" Callie said. "Desperate times call for desperate measures."

I wasn't so sure about that. Even if Mr. Henshaw had

lost his mind and decided to slash his way to the top, Regent Maximus was so far behind in the competition that Mr. Henshaw would have to cut off more than a few Unicorn tails to even stand a chance.

That was what I told myself, at least.

The doorbell rang, and Callie leaped happily. "That's the pizza. Put those fire lizards away and come have dinner. We've all got a long day tomorrow."

A Unicorn criminal *and* getting Regent Maximus through round two? Callie was right—tomorrow was going to be a *really* long day.

CHAPTER 12

Everyone Likes Baby Unicorns

The next morning, it was obvious that everyone was a bit nervous in the Unicorn area of the show building, given the events of the night before. Owners were fussing over their Unicorns' already-perfect manes. Handlers were checking and rechecking halters. Unicorns were speaking faster, more frantically—their steady stream of self-compliments felt more forced than usual.

Regent Maximus didn't seem to know what had happened. Thank goodness. He'd never agree to come out of his stall for round two if he thought there was a tail thief on the loose. So now Tomas applied yet more gauze to Regent Maximus's stall walls while I showed the Unicorn the Trident bulletin.

The obstacles in round two would be chosen randomly the morning of, but the bulletin detailed all the things they *could* be, like a number of jumps, a ring search, a shallow pool of water, and even a hoop that had to be jumped through. I was trying to read it out loud slowly and cheerfully, like it was a picture book.

"Once upon a time there was a Unicorn named Regent Maximus and he saw this first jump and it was pretty low—"

"I'll knock my horn on the bar and it will *fall off*!"

"No, no, it won't. And then the brave, beautiful, strong Unicorn went over two jumps! Then he performed a pirouette—"

"*A PIRATE?*"

"A pirouette. It's just a little turn in a circle."

"I'll fall over and fracture my leg and it'll be the end!"

"You won't fracture your leg."

Tomas looked up as he went back to his bag for another roll of gauze. "I read that a Unicorn fractured two legs in the International Cup in Munich."

"He *won't* fracture his leg," I said firmly. "Then the Unicorn smiled and pranced—"

"Hey, guys, how is Regent Maximus today?" Marisol joined us inside the stall. She was wearing a pink EverSun shirt today, and her hair was in a high tidy ponytail. She always managed to look one step tidier than I did.

"We were just preparing for the next round of the Trident. We're a little worried about Regent Maximus getting through it."

"*What?*" Regent Maximus wailed in alarm. "You don't think I'll *survive* it?"

Of course, Marisol just heard a bunch of panicked whinnying. She patted his shoulder and asked, "Hey—did you hear about Silver Stables's Unicorn?"

"My cousin told me last night! I can't believe someone would cut off a—um . . ." I looked at Regent Maximus and smiled nicely. "I can't believe something like that would happen." The last thing I wanted Regent Maximus to hear was that someone had cut off a Unicorn's tail.

"They're really upset. He was a very promising show Unicorn, and tails take a very long time to grow. He might be too old to show by the time it's all grown out," Marisol said sadly. "Poor thing."

"Maybe he can take the time to relax," Tomas said helpfully. "I bet it's pretty stressful to be a show Unicorn, with all the grooming and glitter and competition. Stress is terrible for your health, you know. It causes ulcers."

Marisol considered this. "I'm not so sure. These Unicorns are *made* to show. They love it." Her eyes drifted to Regent Maximus. There was an ant crawling along the edge of the stall, and the Unicorn was frozen, eyes wide, watching it fearfully. "Well, most of them. Is he afraid of that bug?"

"Yep," I said. "Though it might be the wood. He's afraid of wood too."

"Wood is *everywhere*," Regent Maximus whispered in response, not taking his eyes off the ant.

"Hm," Marisol said. "He's so high-strung! I guess the honeysuckle bedding can't fix everything. Wait, I know something that might help. Do you know how he does with other Unicorns?"

"I think he's as afraid of them as he is of everything else," I said with a shrug.

"I have an idea, then!" Marisol said, a little louder than normal. She looked excited. I could tell that she was in danger of getting carried away, but she reined herself back in. "Sometimes we do it with our own Unicorns, if they're a little stressed. Let's go for a walk."

Marisol took the three of us—me (holding a lead rope), Tomas (applying lotion around his own nostrils), and Regent Maximus (wearing Prince Temujin's scarf over his eyes)—to a very sturdily fenced area near the center ring labeled EVERSUN UNICORN NURSERY.

"Baby Unicorns?" Tomas asked, putting the lid back on the lotion.

"Sometimes high-strung animals do better around babies," Marisol said.

"Oh!" I said. "Regent Maximus, I think you might like this!"

Marisol pushed open the gate, and the Unicorn nursery came into view. The ground was covered in a combination of lavender, hay, and honeysuckle. The wooden walls were painted pale purple, and there were signs hung up on the sides: ANDERSON BRAND HONEY-MILK: ONLY THE BEST FOR YOUR BOTTLE-FED UNICORN! and ADDITIVE-FREE HOOF POLISH: SAFE FOR GROWING HOOVES! There was a long, low trough full of honeycomb that'd been cut into tiny pieces, and a few fluffy blankets wrapped up like nests in one corner.

And there were baby Unicorns!

Baby.

Unicorns.

Six of them, playing some sort of tag-prance-wrestling game with one another.

"Aren't they cute?" Marisol said, lighting up. She bit her lip excitedly. "That one there, the blue-purple one? I bottle raised her. I'm going to show her next year! And I think we might try to do therapy work with her too, if we can just get her permitted so hospitals will let her in. Visiting with Unicorns is proven to strengthen people's immune systems!" Marisol said all this so fast that I could barely understand her. She was like a completely different person than she had been in school, where she always spoke distinctly and politely, as if she had thought through every word. I liked *carried away* Marisol so much better than school Marisol.

"I didn't know that!" I said, delighted to have something so great to add to the Unicorn page of the *Guide*.

"If that's true, I'm gonna visit a lot of Unicorns," Tomas said.

Marisol waved her arms so enthusiastically that I was glad Regent Maximus was still blindfolded. "It's true! It's where the myth about Unicorns being able to heal illness comes from. They can't do that exactly, but they definitely help. Did you know the larger varieties of Unicorns can be trained for high-altitude search and rescue? They're teamed up with a Pegasus, and the Unicorn works on the ground while the Pegasus is in the air!"

Whoa—I'd known there were a few different varieties of Unicorns, but I'd never heard about the search-and-rescue thing. I made a mental note to add that to the *Guide* too.

"What's going on?" Regent Maximus muttered to me.

"We've found you some friends," I told him. "Should I take off his blindfold, Marisol?"

"Yep yep!" Marisol replied, unclipping Regent Maximus's lead as I removed the scarf.

The Unicorn in Infancy

Juvenile Unicorns are different from adults in several significant ways. If a Unicorn has any of the items on this list, it is under six months old:

- curly mane & tail
- rubbery horn to prevent injury
- no teeth
- fruity scent that matches its mother's for identification

Regent Maximus was so startled by the sudden brightness that he fell back and sat down like a dog. This attracted the attention of the baby Unicorns, who abandoned their game. They raced over to stand in a semicircle around us, staring at Regent Maximus with giant, questioning eyes as he clambered to his feet again.

"Hello!" one said, stamping a fuzzy foot on the ground. It pranced down in a play bow. When Regent Maximus didn't return the move, it tilted its head to the side. "Hey? Hello! Greetings! Hi!"

"Maybe he can't hear us," a watermelon pink baby Unicorn suggested.

"Or maybe he doesn't speak our language! Maybe he only speaks Griffin! Maybe he was *raised by Griffins*!" a blue one said excitedly, and they all cheered at the prospect.

I wanted to assure the baby Unicorns that Regent Maximus could hear them and had not been raised by Griffins, so far as I knew. But I wasn't so sure about talking to magical creatures in front of Marisol. Regent Maximus, thankfully, spoke up.

"Hello," he said in a low voice.

"Hi! Were you raised by Griffins?" the pink one asked.

Regent Maximus looked shocked. "Griffins? Griffins eat chicken cutlets. Unicorns can't chew chicken cutlets. You could choke on them."

The baby Unicorns looked perplexed. Regent Maximus looked at me somewhat desperately.

I cleared my throat and said, "Regent Maximus met a baby Grim this year."

Marisol was impressed, if a bit confused, by this sudden announcement. "Really?"

The baby Unicorns also shouted, *"Really?"* all at the same time. Impressed, they gathered up close around Regent Maximus, who seemed a little bewildered. He nodded.

"Grims are supposed to be very dangerous, you know. You can't just be friends with any old Grim," Regent Maximus warned them.

"Then how did you become his friend?" a sage-green baby Unicorn asked breathlessly.

"Oh, well, I—" Regent Maximus began, but then glanced at me. I motioned for him to go on. "Well, you see, it started when my barn turned into a *blazing inferno*! I was trapped in my stall, with *no escape in sight* . . ."

The eyes of the baby Unicorns went wide and, one by one, they each plopped onto the ground, eager to hear Regent Maximus's rather overdramatic version of the story. Marisol and I slowly backed out of the pen, nearly crashing into Tomas, who, to my surprise, was already waiting outside, looking at a bulletin for the Rockshine show classes.

"What?" he asked when I pointed at the bulletin, mouth hanging open.

"There are baby Unicorns *right there*, and you're looking at Rockshine pictures?"

"Unicorns are fine, but Rockshines are my favorite. Can we go see them again now?"

Marisol glanced at me. I could tell she wasn't any more interested in Rockshines than I was. "I can't go with you. I have to meet up with my sisters. We have to take care of our Unicorns because Dad was out so late last night at the barn, working on the truck and trailer or something. But maybe we can talk later? I've got a few ideas for getting Regent Maximus through round two of the Trident."

"We'll take all the help we can get," I said. I felt bad, though, because the first thing I'd thought of after she said the part about her dad was how *someone* had been cutting Unicorn tails off the night before, and it wasn't too far from the truck parking lot to where the Unicorns were kept. After she left, I asked, "Tomas, before we go see the Rockshines, would you mind a short detour? An *investigative* detour."

"What are we investigating?"

"A Unicorn got his tail cut off last night, Tomas. So we're going to go ask him who did it."

CHAPTER
— 13 —

To Catch a Tail Thief

First stop: Unicorns.

"Let's see, Forever Sunshine, Forever Sunshine, where is Forever Sunshine," I said, walking down the hall and reading names off the stall doors. "Porcelain Promise, Little Miss Jupiter, Lavender Loyalty . . ." Tomas trailed behind me with a notebook and pen, prepared to take notes on our findings. He had immediately warmed to our task: If there was anything Tomas liked, it was a job.

"Here!" I stopped by the name plaque and peered in the stall. Empty!

The pale green Unicorn in the next stall over was sharpening his horn on the metal track of his stall door, but he stopped when I said, "Excuse me—I'm looking for Forever Sunshine. Do you know where he is?"

"Oh! It was terrible. So terrible!" the green Unicorn said. "Sunshine was so beautiful!"

"I'm sure he's still beautiful," I said. "Where is he? I wanted to talk to him, to see if he knows who cut his tail."

The green Unicorn turned in a little nervous circle. "He's home, hiding his shame. He left this morning."

I gave Tomas a frustrated look. He scribbled *went home* in his notepad. I asked, "Did he say anything about who cut his tail?"

The Unicorn shook his head, a frenzy of bright blue mane. "He didn't see. We were all getting our beauty sleep! Just between you and me, he needed it. Do you see how much sleep I've gotten? Do you see how beautiful I am?"

The Unicorn stuck his head over the stall door and shoved his nose in my face.

"Oh, yes. Um. Very beautiful. Anyhow—do you know *anything* about the person who cut his tail?"

The Unicorn pulled his head back in and turned to look in his water bucket, where he could see his own reflection. "The person ran off toward the Griffins. You there. Small boy. Do you think I've gotten enough beauty sleep? Ask him if he thinks I'm beautiful."

Tomas didn't understand, of course. He just stood there with his pencil hovering over his paper.

"Tell him to draw a picture of me," the Unicorn continued. "My left side. That's my most beautiful side."

"Maybe later," I said. "Thanks for your help."

Second stop: Griffins.

I thought Standard Griffins were pretty cool, but I could tell right away that Tomas was nervous. I didn't blame him. He was very short, and they were very tall. And they squeaked and snapped and cawed at one another through the stall doors and walls, shouting things like "You there!" and "I'm twice the eagle you are!" and "We'll settle this with fisticuffs!"

"I read that Standard Griffins can take a man's arm off," Tomas whispered to me. "I don't have anything in my bag for that."

"Can't you just keep your arms out of their stalls?" I asked.

"In the Middle Ages, they *ate* children," Tomas said, a little louder to be heard over their noisy sparring.

"We're not *in* the Middle Ages," I replied. "And these are domesticated. Do you have any mint in your bag? I heard that mint makes them calm down."

"I have a menthol rub in case I get a chest cold before tonight," Tomas said. He dug the little pot of mint-scented cream out of his bag. The moment he opened the lid, all of the Griffins slowly fell quiet, turning their attention to us.

I had to admit that even I felt a little anxious with all of their stern faces suddenly turned to me.

"Well then," I said, clasping my hands together. "We just need a moment of your time. Last night a Unicorn's tail was cut off—someone was trying to sabotage his show chances. One of the Unicorns said he saw the culprit run this way. Did any of you see anything?"

"Last night?" echoed the largest of them. His plaque said that his name was General. He clicked his beak in thought. "You know, I did see something. A man. Around the time Felix and Transistor were talking about arm wrestling?"

"But . . . Griffins don't have arms, really," I pointed out.

"As if that could stop us!" one of the other Griffins said.

"What did he look like?" I asked.

"He was dressed in black," General replied.

Tomas wrote this down, his handwriting a little wobbly and nervous.

"I saw him too!" a Griffin shouted from another stall. "He was very tall. Almost as tall as long-legs Lucretia over there."

"What did you just call me?" Lucretia barked from

yet another stall. "Say it to my face—oh, wait! You can't reach my face, stub-legs!"

This set off another round of shouting and tussling and yet more shouting. Feathers flew from stalls and Griffins laughed and cajoled and kicked at their stall walls. Tomas waved the pot of menthol with a nervous hand, but it had no effect whatsoever.

I turned to Tomas. "Let's get out of here."

Third stop: Exhibition Hall.

If I were running from the Unicorn Hall through the Griffin stables, it would be the next step on the journey. We hadn't yet been to the Exhibition Hall, even though I'd marked it as a "Definite Priority!" on our list of things to see. It contained all of the noncompeting magical creatures—creatures like Flowerbeasts or Gipybieras, who were fascinating, but not common enough to have enough animals for a contest.

The hall was packed with people. It would be difficult to have a real conversation with any of the creatures here. We tried to pick a pen without too many spectators and found ourselves by the Dillopods.

The Dillopods had been all rolled up on themselves, but as we approached, one unwound. Its body was pale yellow and soft-looking.

Standard Griffin

Standard Griffins possess teeth in addition to sharp beaks

Unlike most winged animals, Griffins do not fly instinctually; they must be taught by their mothers or they will never fly

A steady diet of sardines and carrots will produce a glorious coat but very bad breath

Some Griffins fall ill with Janus Syndrome, where the eagle half argues with the lion half. Janus Syndrome is treated with a diet of mint leaves

---

SIZE: 7-9'

WEIGHT: 1,000-1,250 lbs.

DESCRIPTION: Standard Griffins are the largest of the Griffins ever since the Giant Banded Griffin went extinct in 1921. These enthusiastic animals are best kept as only pets, as their good-natured sparring will quickly wreak havoc in most households. In the wild, Griffins will often battle together for hours on end. Although these fights look fierce, they are usually joyful and the Griffins' tough hides mean there are few injuries.

"Hi there," I said cheerfully. "I'm Pip, and this is my friend Tomas. I was wondering—late last night, did you happen to see a tall man dressed in black around here after everyone else was gone?"

The Dillopod curled back into a ball. I thought this meant the conversation was over, but he merely rolled over to the others, knocking into them like pool balls until they all uncurled and looked up at me.

"She wants to know if we saw a tall man dressed in black?" the first asked.

"We did!" another said. "We saw him last night, late, right after we finished our exercises."

"Oh, that's right! We did four laps and push-ups and then stacks," another said.

"Stacks?" I asked.

The Dillopods responded by curling up again, then rolling into and over one another, until they were arranged in a perfect little pyramid of spheres. Tomas stuck the notepad under his arm so he could clap for them; he obviously vastly preferred them to the Griffins. The Dillopods trilled in appreciation before collapsing neatly back to the floor.

"Yes, we saw him," one—the first one? They all looked just alike—told us. "He was carrying a big orange thing—"

"The Unicorn tail!" I explained. "Tomas, they saw him!"

The Dillopods continued. "He had shiny shoes. Like our backs."

I turned to tell Tomas this and discovered that he was glowing. He was now the same pale yellow color as the Dillopods' skin and twice as bright. He was a Tomas lightbulb.

"I guess my allergy pill doesn't cover Dillopods," Tomas said, turning his hand back and forth in front of his face.

"Does it hurt?" I asked.

"No," Tomas said. "But I hope it wears off before I get home."

He had begun to attract the attention of other spectators. A man wandered closer from the Pixtail pen. "Hey! You're glowing! Susan, come look! This boy is glowing!"

"Just allergic to Dillopods!" Tomas explained.

"Look at the boy over there! He's glowing!" someone else said.

"Can we get our picture with you? Do you always glow, or only for special occasions?" a woman asked.

"Just allergic—" Tomas tried again, but people were excited now.

"Have you considered caving? You wouldn't need to carry a lantern."

DILLOPOD

Ears can rotate
in a complete circle

Thick hide protects them
from snakes, birds, and
domesticated dogs,
who regularly mistake
curled Dillopods for
tennis balls

Claws can displace
30 lb of dirt, rock,
or tile flooring
in under ten minutes

Dillopods will often begin to roll in their
sleep, and hundreds of them are often
found piled, still sleeping, in ravines
and drainage ditches during the summer months

IZE: 4-7"

EIGHT: 11-15 oz.

ESCRIPTION: Dillopods have a mysterious
amily structure. They seem to function
s a cohesive unit rather than a collection
f individuals. While they are attractive
ets, remember that breaking up a Dillopod
amily is irresponsible; be prepared to
ake the entire Cluster if you want one.

"My friend would love to get a photo with you!"

"Have you always glowed, or did you choose this recently?"

Tomas's eyes were getting enormous. And they were glowing too so he looked like some kind of magical creature himself. It was definitely time to get out of here. I grabbed Tomas's backpack strap. "Sorry, everyone," I said, "we have to go!"

We *ran*.

Fourth stop: . . . somewhere.

I couldn't really tell where we'd ended up. There were no animals in this area, just bales and bales of lavender and hay and lilacs stacked beside giant bags of feed—honey and oat feed for Pegasi, rock salt and coal for Manticores, and the less appealing sardines and carrots for the Standard Griffins. Farther down, there were sealed bins as tall as me labeled HONEYCOMB, LIVER, and ORANGES.

Both Tomas and I jumped when we heard a voice behind us.

"Sorry, but this area is off-limits to spectat—oh! Pip Bartlett, right?" It was Mr. Barrera. He stood near the feed hall entrance, looking quite tidy in a suit and tie. Unicorn handlers often dress up to be as fancy as their charges, but most people don't wear their fancy clothing while moving hay, which was what Mr. Barrera seemed to be doing. Like Marisol, though, he somehow managed to stay clean while doing dirty work.

"Yeah," I said. "And this is Tomas."

Tomas had stopped glowing and was now carefully cleaning between his fingers with a sanitary wipe.

"What're you doing in here? Marisol tells me you love magical creatures—but there aren't any back here. Just food!"

"Oh! I do love them. But there was just . . . well . . . Tomas here was . . . we're just taking a break," I said.

"It can be a touch overwhelming sometimes, even for those of us who do a lot of shows," Mr. Barrera agreed. He grabbed one of the red food buckets off a hook near the door. As he passed us, he scooped up a big bucket of honeysuckle. "Well, I hope you enjoy the show! See you around, Pip!"

Well! I had to admit that even though Marisol wasn't mad at me about the Unicorn Incident last year, I'd sort of thought Mr. Barrera might still be. But he didn't seem mad at all.

"*His* shoes sure were shiny," Tomas said, in a meaningful voice.

I made a face. But he was right—Mr. Barerra's shoes

were very shiny, just how the Dillopods described the tail thief's shoes. And Mr. Barrera had easily grabbed the red feed bucket off the hook . . . because he was very tall. And Marisol had said that her father was out late the night before.

No. *No.* He couldn't have been the one to cut Forever Sunshine's tail. I said, "No way."

"He *would* have a good reason to do it, though. Doesn't this mean one of his Unicorns is more likely to win?"

"Yes, but . . . it can't be him! Besides, it's not as if he's the only tall man in shiny shoes around here!" Though there were not many people who wore fancy shoes to a dusty Unicorn show.

"True. There's also Mr. Henshaw," Tomas said sadly.

"There could be someone else," I replied. "There are lots of people here."

Tomas didn't look particularly convinced. And the truth was, I wasn't particularly convinced either.

CHAPTER 14

Regent Maximus's Guide to Survival

Even though the Unicorn-tail investigation had been more discouraging than anything else, things were looking up on the Regent Maximus front.

He spent most of the day in the Unicorn nursery, and it made him into a completely different Unicorn! Well. Almost. He was still overdramatic. But the baby Unicorns thought he was incredibly brave, because Regent Maximus's stories made it sound like he was moments from disaster at every turn. And he seemed to be gathering confidence by teaching them what he knew . . . even if I thought that the skills he offered were not the most useful skills possible for baby Unicorns. For instance, when we arrived at the Unicorn nursery to work with him on round-two training, I found him saying to them, "Today, we will be discussing *explosions*."

"Regent Maximus, what are you doing?" I asked, as Marisol and Tomas discussed how to transform the nursery into a practice ring.

"I've been teaching them *survival skills*, Pip," Regent Maximus said. He turned back to the babies. "Having made it through many, many explosions or near-explosions myself, I am something of an expert. Here is the secret: When you think something *might* explode, or if something *does* explode, or if you have a dream about something exploding, you want to GET DOWN! COVER YOUR HORN!"

Regent Maximus shouted the last bit so loud the baby Unicorns reared back in surprise. Swiftly, he dropped to the ground and curled into a ball with his horn hidden among his legs. The baby Unicorns shrieked and copied him. They stayed that way for a moment, and then I heard Regent Maximus whisper from between his hooves.

"And make sure you stay here, since some kinds of explosions take a long time—like Manticores, right, Pip?"

Manticores *did* tend to release explosive balls of fire in intervals, according to the *Guide*. I thought that perhaps I shouldn't read the *Guide* when Regent Maximus could look over my shoulder anymore.

"Uh, that's right," I said. Regent Maximus gave a satisfied snort.

"Pip knows *everything* about dangerous magical creatures, class. Pay attention to her warnings," Regent Maximus said. The baby Unicorns muttered in agreement.

"Now we're going to talk about avoiding *asteroids* falling from the sky."

I thought about stopping him, but really, it wouldn't hurt to have him distracted as we set up the course. I left him demonstrating how to roll away from space debris and joined Marisol and Tomas in transforming the nursery. The idea was to make a course like the one Regent Maximus might face in round two. We took two of the signs off the wall and planted them in the ground as jumps, and Tomas and I used empty feed buckets to create the barrel-weave section. Marisol, Tomas, and I all strained our muscles to pull a water trough into the middle of the nursery to be like the possible water jump.

"All right," Marisol said, hands on her hips. "Let's saddle him up!"

Regent Maximus's brave face slipped when he saw Marisol hauling his saddle off the fence. He turned his head so the baby Unicorns couldn't hear and whispered, "Oh oh oh, is she going to put that on my back?"

"Yes, but it's very light. More like a blanket," I assured him. "Tomas, do you have a saddle safety fact?"

"They're designed for Unicorn bone structure," Tomas said. "I read the federal guideline sticker on the bottom of the saddle just now. It meets all safety regulations for your back muscles."

I translated. Regent Maximus sucked in his lips, then looked over his shoulder. The baby Unicorns were all gathered in their blanket nests, sitting on their haunches and watching eagerly, looking away only to nip a snack of honeycomb from the little pile we'd left each of them.

This steeled Regent Maximus. He released his lips with a *phhbbbbbblllllllltttttt* sound. "Okay. Okay okay okay, I'll try. Can you check the saddle for lake fleas, though?"

"We're nowhere near a lake, though, so there can't be any lake fleas—"

"I checked it when I was reading the label. No lake fleas," Tomas interrupted. When I stared at him, he said, "What? Lake fleas can carry seventeen diseases transmittable to humans. And also they spread quickly among Rockshines. I didn't want to accidentally infest Ms. Gould's herd."

While we were talking, Marisol had effortlessly saddled Regent Maximus without him even noticing. It was really quite clever—she just patted his side again and again and again, until he got used to the feeling of being touched, and then she slid the saddle onto his back in the direction that his hair grew. I made a note to write that into the *Guide*'s section on Unicorn training. Marisol's experience with Unicorns meant I'd made a *lot* of notes since she started helping us.

The crystal bit and bridle were trickier—Regent Maximus shied away, worried he'd choke on the bit or trip on the reins or that the clasps of the bridle would knot in his mane. The baby Unicorns cheered when the bridle was finally in place.

"Can you give me a leg up?" Marisol asked. She was the obvious choice to ride him during the practice, since she had actual experience riding Unicorns (my time riding a Unicorn in a stampede didn't count). Once she was on, Tomas and I went to sit near the baby Unicorns.

"Here he goes! Here he goes!" the watermelon-pink one said, burrowing even tighter in her blanket, like she couldn't handle all the excitement.

"Has he ever told you about the time a HobGrackle tried to eat him?" an orange one asked earnestly. "All the things he's seen! It's amazing!"

Speaking of amazing, I was amazed at the transformation in Regent Maximus. He was still very far from being Jeffrey Higgleston's Ideal Unicorn. But when he'd arrived here, he had been too afraid to really move around without a blindfold, and every time he'd heard the loudspeaker, he'd begun to shake. Now he allowed Marisol to guide him slowly around the obstacle course so that he could get a good look at everything. He was crawling low enough that her feet dragged on the ground sometimes, but he still let her convince him to examine every obstacle without closing his eyes. And when a loudspeaker crackle made him startle and accidentally jump one of the jumps, he didn't immediately run for cover. Instead, he shot a glance at the baby Unicorns, who looked at him in awe. He did his best to look like he'd meant to do it. Of course, he still wouldn't purposefully *jump* over them when Marisol rode him toward one, opting instead to do a sort of climb-scramble-hop. It wasn't graceful, but it was pretty good—for Regent Maximus.

The baby Unicorns were thrilled.

"I didn't know you could *climb* the jumps!" one squealed.

"He just looks at the world so differently!" another said, sighing admiringly.

Even with all the climbing and slithering, I was pretty proud of Regent Maximus, and told him so, as Marisol dismounted.

"I did good? Really?" he said, like he thought I might be lying.

"You did *great*. Just make sure you're as nice to Mr. Henshaw as you were to Marisol. Remember that Mr. Henshaw isn't such an experienced rider, okay?"

Marisol had been rubbing down his coat where the saddle had been, but when she heard her name, she grinned at me. She had never asked why I talked to animals, because she talked to them all the time too. The big difference was that she didn't seem to expect them to answer her. She went back to rubbing his coat and said, "Sometimes I wish they could understand us. Imagine how much easier that would make this!"

"Er," I said.

"Person," Regent Maximus warned me. "Person person person."

I followed his gaze to the nursery door and felt a little nervous jolt in my stomach. Prince Temujin stood there, looking at Regent Maximus with a thoughtful expression. "Excuse me, I don't mean to disturb your training. I just find his rainbow mane and tail so very striking. And I see that he is really coming along, isn't he? With Forever Sunshine and Porcelain Promise out of the running, your Unicorn here might not do so badly after all!"

"Porcelain Promise is out of the running?" Marisol asked.

"His owners decided to withdraw him from the competition. Too risky, they said, to have their champion here with such poor security." Prince Temujin sounded disappointed. "I see from your shirt that you're with EverSun—one of the Barrera daughters? I suppose this means your girl Duchess could win the Trident!"

"I suppose so," Marisol said, but she didn't look very happy about it. I looked at Prince Temujin. Did he think Marisol's family was involved with the tail cutting, to better Duchess's chances? It was hard to tell. I wanted to ask—I bet a grown-up's opinion on the whole thing would help—but knew I couldn't with Marisol standing right there.

"I just can't believe anyone would want to win that badly!" she said.

Prince Temujin looked as if he had just tasted something unpleasant. "Desperate people sometimes have to do desperate things, I suppose. And the tails *do* grow back, after all, if a bit slowly. There's really no need to panic."

I wasn't as sure, and from the looks of it, neither was Marisol.

Prince Temjuin drummed his fingers against the fence. "This Unicorn certainly is magnificent. He would be quite a lovely specimen for Galatolia's depleted herds."

In all of the other fuss, I had nearly forgotten that we had to worry about Mr. Henshaw selling Regent Maximus. From the look on Tomas's face, he had too.

Surely Mr. Henshaw wouldn't sell him now, though. Regent Maximus was going to make it through round two. He had to.

CHAPTER
— 15 —

Heeeeeeeeeyyyyyyyyyyyyy, Part Three

I felt like I'd only been asleep for a few minutes that night when Callie woke me by kicking the side of my bed.

"Get up," she said. She sounded too sleepy to be cranky. "We have to go on a call with Mom."

I opened my eyes. It looked as dark with them open as with them closed. "Am I awake?"

Callie pulled off my blanket, still with the same slow sleepiness. She muttered, "Now you are," before stumbling back out of my room like a zombie.

Downstairs, I found Aunt Emma already all packed up with her vet bag. Callie leaned against her with a level of snuggliness that she would have never shown while awake. Aunt Emma patted her hair and then said, "Sorry, guys. But I don't feel comfortable leaving you here alone."

I sat in the front seat because Callie wanted to lie down in the back. I was wide-awake; the strangeness of being woken had driven sleep from me.

"What's going on?" I asked.

"Mariah called me," Aunt Emma replied. "One of the Rockshines is sick."

Tomas wouldn't be happy to hear that.

At the showgrounds, we found the parking lot empty, and when we got out of the car, night bugs buzzed and frogs sang gleefully. Overhead, a GrowlOwl swept low, growling like a wildcat as it did. I jumped, but Callie didn't—her eyes were closed as she gave an enormous yawn. Inside the building was actually quieter than the outside, with no sounds except for the snuffling and snoring and drowsy chattering of animals in their stalls.

"What's that?" I whispered. Up ahead, lights were flashing from behind one of the removable curtain walls between animal sections. Sound went along with it too. It sounded a little like . . . drums.

Aunt Emma looked mystified. Together we crept forward. The sound grew louder, and now we could see that the lights were different colors. They seemed to be flashing in time with the drumming. When we got to the edge of the curtain, we saw the source of the sound: The Blankbirds were having a dance party! A few male Blankbirds were projecting a variety of colored lights on a few females, who were drumming a festive beat against the rafters and pipes hanging from the ceiling. The rest of the Blankbirds strutted across the concrete floor.

They all saw us at the same time. Several dozen Blankbirds froze, staring at us, and then the entire area went dark.

"Nothing to see here!" one Blankbird said in the black.

"Just us Blankbirds, looking for . . . uh . . . spilled popcorn!" another said.

"Yep, yep, spilled popcorn!"

Of course, everyone else heard only chirping. Callie muttered, "That was weird. Am I awake?"

"Sort of," said Aunt Emma, placing a hand on her shoulder to guide her to the Glimmerbeast area.

"Heyyyy," said one of the Rockshines, in a tired way.

"Heeyy," said another agreeably. I thought it might be Bucky, the Rockshine I'd first met at the clinic, but to be honest they all sort of looked the same, especially in this dim light.

Ms. Gould said, "Thank you for coming so late, Emma."

Callie made a snuffling noise, pulled her hood up, and curled up on a pile of quilted blankets that were normally for the Rockshines.

"You can sit over there too, if you like," Aunt Emma told me.

"No, I'm okay," I replied. "Can I help?"

Ms. Gould laughed quietly, so as not to disturb the sleeping animals. "This one's a live one!"

"She sure is," Aunt Emma replied. "Okay, let's see this gal."

We moved around to where Ms. Gould had trapped a Rockshine in a metal, roofless cage. The animal didn't look happy to me, but Rockshines never really did.

"Oh, I see," Aunt Emma said immediately. "Do you have any honeysuckle here, Mariah?"

"Oh, no, I'm just out. Do you need me to get some?"

"Hm," Aunt Emma said. "I actually need you to hold her for me, I think. Pip, do you mind terribly getting some honeysuckle from the Unicorn area? We can replace it in the morning."

It was dark, but the animals would be making comforting noises all around me.

"Okay," I said. "How much?"

"A little bale. Maybe this big?" Aunt Emma made a gesture with her hands.

I set off through the dark arena, pattering as quietly as I could. As I got to the Unicorn area, I could hear that the Unicorns were already awake. They were making scuffling, alarmed noises.

At first I thought that maybe *I* had been the one to

startle them, so I opened my mouth to say something comforting, but then I heard the words of the loudest Unicorn.

"Back! Back, you fiend! *Back!*" a Unicorn shouted. It was Fortnight, one of the Barreras' Unicorns I'd met before, during the Unicorn Incident.

I closed my mouth and crept closer to his stall. I couldn't see much, because it was dark, but I saw enough to see that Fortnight was spinning in his stall.

"Never!" His voice was panicked. "Fight back, Duchess! But try not to damage your coat! They'll never be able to glossy it up by tomorrow if you do! And who are you without your beauty? WHO ARE ANY OF US?"

I was right next to Fortnight's stall and still couldn't see any details. I could hear the Unicorn in the next stall over—Duchess—scuffling around in her stall, though.

"Fortnight!" I whispered. "What's wrong?"

"Oh, hurrah! It's you, grimy child! Save Duchess!" he said.

"From *what*?"

"A monster!"

I didn't believe there was a monster. But I did believe that Duchess was terrified of something. I did the only thing I could think of:

I went to the end of the hall and hit the light switch.

Light filled the aisles and I froze in place, my fingers still on the switch.

It was no monster. It was *a person*. A tall man wearing a ski mask and shiny shoes, a pair of scissors in one hand and a freshly chopped tail in the other. He was all hunched over, looking about as surprised and scared as I felt.

"No!" I shouted. "What are you doing! Stop!"

All the Unicorns began to shout too. "Stop! Stop! Don't worry, Duchess! She's here to save our beauty!"

The scissors clattered on the floor, but the man stopped to scrape them up. I saw just his shoulder as he scrambled out of the stall and away—with a beautiful length of Unicorn tail trailing from his hands.

I was too late. Duchess's tail was gone.

CHAPTER
— 16 —

Things Get a Little Fishy

One tail chop was a scandal, but two tail chops? That was *scary*. The police were called. The Unicorn owners were called. I had to give a full report of what I had seen. As Callie had said earlier: Scandal! Scandal! Scandal! It didn't take long for Unicorn owners to begin to appear at the barn, even though it was still barely morning. The Barreras were some of the first to arrive—Mr. Barrera was still in a pair of plaid pajama bottoms, with no sign of the fancy clothing he'd been wearing during the day. No fancy shoes. Surely that meant he wasn't the tail thief. Plus, why would he cut one of his own Unicorn's tails? Everyone else seemed relieved too, as they arrived, like they had also possibly suspected the Barreras.

Marisol was beside herself over the crime. She was less concerned with Duchess's show chances than with Duchess's mood, which was in the pits. She was just shouting, "I'm not beautiful!" over and over again.

"Who would *do* this?" Marisol wailed.

As the sun finally came up, there was one Unicorn owner who was still not at the barn: Mr. Henshaw.

I wanted to believe that the man in the ski mask wasn't him, but the truth was, I couldn't really say for sure.

Thankfully, it seemed like the police were now taking over the investigation for me. Two new officers had arrived at the barn and had asked everyone involved with the Unicorns to form a line for some data gathering.

Even though I'd already been interviewed, I had to stand in line too, right behind Aunt Emma, at the very end. When we got up to the front, I found out that one of the officers was holding an orange bucket full of water labeled POLICE. A distinctly fishy odor was coming from the water. Not entirely pleasant. Actually, entirely unpleasant.

I saw now that there was something besides water in the bucket: a bunch of Wimpelings. I knew about Wimpelings from both the *Guide to Magical Creatures* and the beaches in Savannah.

One of the officers removed a Wimpeling from the bucket, stuck it onto the wall (it made a *sqwlick!* sound), and then pulled it off (*sqwlick!*). She handed it to the other officer, who recorded something on a digital tablet. Then they did it again. I badly wanted to ask them what they were doing with the Wimpeling, but I didn't know if it

Wimpleling

Wimplelings are thought to possess the most powerful sense of smell in the Magical Creature world

During "slime season," Wimplelings emit a smelly, oozy substance through their pores to attract a potential mate

The Wimpleling is equally at home in and out of the water, hopping on land and propelling itself with gas bubbles in the ocean

Lacking bones, Wimplelings are able to rearrange their body parts, including their eyes, into whichever location is most convenient

---

SIZE: 12-24"

WEIGHT: 1-2 lbs.

DESCRIPTION: Originally known as the "Sea Glob," the Wimpleling was renamed after Paula Wimpleling, the police officer who discovered their use in police work. Often used as an inexpensive and hypoallergenic alternative to police dogs, Wimplelings have the downside of being unattractive on parade floats and difficult to pin medals on.

would somehow interfere with the investigation or just be distracting while they were doing serious police work.

Luckily for me, my aunt is a lot like me, because as she held her hand out to them, she said, "I've never seen Wimpelings used for this before! Is it because of their sense of smell? Pardon my questions; I'm a vet for magical creatures and I just don't see a lot of sea creatures at the practice."

"Not a problem," replied the first officer. She stuck the Wimpeling to Aunt Emma's hand (*sqwlick!*), pulled it off (*sqwlick!*), and handed it to the other officer. "As you already know, Wimpelings are excellent at picking up smells, which often stick around even when there's no other evidence left. So we stick them over the door handle of the stall where the affected Unicorn was—see, like this—" She fetched one out and stuck it on the stall door. Water oozed off the Wimpeling . . . or *out of* the Wimpeling. "You see where the edge of the Wimpeling's trumpet attaches to the surface? See how it's starting to wrinkle? It is making a very specific shape in response to this specific odor. It's as specific as a fingerprint."

She pulled the Wimpeling off the door (*sqwlick!*) and handed it to the other officer, who stuck it to his tablet to record the odor. "When we find a suspect, we'll match his or her scent to our records."

"Are there any suspects?" I asked, wide-eyed, as she plopped the Wimpeling into the bucket.

"This is my niece," Aunt Emma said proudly, putting her arm over my shoulders. "You don't have to answer if it's against procedure or whatever."

"It's all right to ask. No, not yet. But it's important to collect the data now, just in case," she said. "Wimpelings are incredibly accurate, and unlike computers and databases, they can't crash or be hacked."

"Oh!" I said.

"Probably not as fluffy as the magical creatures you're used to, huh?" she asked, smiling at me.

"No, but I like all magical creatures. Even the . . . er . . . gooey ones."

The police officers seemed pleased by this answer. They swirled around the Wimpelings in the bucket to make sure they were all submerged, and then put the top on it tightly.

"Try not to worry," the first police officer told us. "We'll get this figured out."

As they headed down the aisle, I heard the second police officer say, "I'm going to smell like fish all day."

Everyone in the Unicorn hall watched them go; the moment they were out of sight, everyone got right back to work—Unicorns had to be groomed and saddled for round two of the Trident.

The show must go on, after all.

CHAPTER
17

Round Two

We were all a little bleary-eyed the rest of the day. Aunt Emma staggered off with coffee; Callie sat motionless with a soda in her hand. I kept my energy up by staying focused on the goal: Getting Regent Maximus through round two. Mr. Henshaw, Tomas, Regent Maximus, and I were in the baby Unicorn pen. Mr. Henshaw hadn't explained where he was during the investigation earlier, even though I heard him telling Aunt Emma that he was sorry that he hadn't been there for Regent Maximus during all of the commotion. I couldn't decide if I thought that was a nice thing for him to say or if I was too worried that he was a suspect to think it was nice.

It was hard to remember to be entirely suspicious, though, when Mr. Henshaw was trying so hard to prepare for round two. He was currently seated on Regent Maximus, and the two of them had just finished doing a practice run through our homemade obstacles (which meant putting a helmet on Mr. Henshaw and convincing Regent Maximus he didn't need one too).

"Wow, Pip! He's not bad!" Mr. Henshaw said.

"Wow, Pip! He's not bad!" Regent Maximus said at almost the same time.

I had to admit, they were *both* right. Mr. Henshaw clearly wasn't as skilled a rider as Marisol, and Regent Maximus clearly wasn't as confident a creature as the other Unicorns, but they were both far, far better than I had expected. The two of them even looked excited!

"It was really mostly Marisol!" I said. "And the baby Unicorns have helped a lot too," I added, for the babies' benefit. They were Unicorns, after all, and loved to hear nice things about themselves.

"That man looks heavy. Regent Maximus must be *so strong*," one of the baby Unicorns whispered. It turned to me, eyes big and hopeful. "Do you think we can come watch round two?"

I wasn't sure people would think very highly of me trying to guide six baby Unicorns through this crowd. In fact, it sounded like an excellent way to start a second Unicorn Incident. So I said, "I bet if you lean over the fence in the back, you can see the center ring." The babies scrambled to the back wall to confirm that, yes, they could see if they stood on the Rockshine feed buckets we'd used to make Regent Maximus's practice jumps.

"Good luck!" they screamed at Regent Maximus.

"I WILL GO NOBLY!" Regent Maximus shouted back. "REMEMBER ME LIKE THIS, NOT FALLEN!"

"Shh," said Mr. Henshaw. "Settle. Pip, why is he whinnying?"

"He's just saying bye to the babies," I replied. It was close enough to the truth.

We were the first to the center ring, though it didn't take long for the other Unicorns to trickle in. The events of the night before had clearly left both the Unicorns and the owners unsettled.

Marisol came charging up to me at the very last minute, just as I was about to find my way to a seat. I'd never seen Marisol look so . . . well, so much like *me*. Her hair was loose from its bun, and there was lavender dust all over her arms.

"How is Regent Maximus?" she asked, breathless. She threw her arms around me in a hug, which startled and alarmed me. It wasn't till she'd flailed backward that I thought to be pleased that she was happy to see me.

I crossed my arms. "He didn't throw Mr. Henshaw at all this morning, and they went over all the obstacles.

They're both nervous, but I think they're going to have a good time. How's your family?"

"Good, considering what happened," Marisol said, and gestured to them. Her parents looked as disheveled as her—the only member of the family who had managed to stay polished and sparkling was one of Marisol's older sisters, who was seated on Fortnight, waiting to enter the ring for round two.

Like most Unicorns, Fortnight was usually proud and perfect, but today he fidgeted. He kept swishing his tail and tucking it beneath his legs. It was too long for that, though, so he tripped over it again and again, tossing his head as he did.

"Is someone standing watch?" he called out across the building—it sounded like a resonant whinny to all the humans except me. "Is anyone making sure we're *safe*?"

Overhead, the loudspeaker crackled: "We're now beginning round two of the Triple Trident!"

We quickly found a spot near the rail. A pink Unicorn went first, then a pretty lavender one. These Unicorns were just as nervous about tail loss as Fortnight. The lavender Unicorn shied here and there before finally refusing to go over an especially tall jump at the end of the course.

"No! No! I won't! My tail could get caught in it!" she cried as her rider circled back and tried the jump a second time. The crowd clapped politely for her and her rider any-how, but the judges—including Prince Temujin—wrote something on their notepads. From their faces, I guessed it wasn't a good something.

Fortnight was up next, and I cheered loudly alongside Marisol. Her sister and Fortnight rode beautifully—and Fortnight's mood seemed to have recovered, given that he shouted, "I AM THE KING OF EVERYTHING!" as he soared over the final jump.

Then it was Regent Maximus's turn. I glanced toward the nursery and saw the baby Unicorns' heads pressed over their fence, bickering with one another over who had the best view. They cheered—and so did the crowd—as Regent Maximus took a few tentative steps through the gate. Thankfully, the course wasn't *too* tricky; they'd chosen obstacles we'd prepared really well for. Still, Regent Maximus pawed at the ground worriedly.

"Oh, Mr. Henshaw, give him a minute to calm down or he'll bolt," Marisol whispered, pounding her hands on the edge of the rail. We craned our necks to get a better look. *Come on, you two! You can do this!* I thought over and over.

Mr. Henshaw and Regent Maximus took a deep breath at the exact same time, and then Mr. Henshaw urged Regent Maximus into a frolic. It was a nervous sort of frolic, and he was quivering from nose to tail, but *still*.

They climbed over the first jump, then the second. When it came time for Regent Maximus to root out a golden ring, he pranced around the pile, chanting, "Circles! Dizzy! Vertigo! Circles!"

"Does he have the ring yet?" one of the baby Unicorns with a lousy view shouted loud enough that I could hear.

"No! He's looking! He's thinking!" one with a better angle answered.

Regent Maximus nervously knelt down to root for the golden ring. Mr. Henshaw saw it before he did; he guided Regent Maximus toward it. A moment later the ring was spinning and clattering down Regent Maximus's spiral horn. Regent Maximus flinched with shock, and for a second, I thought it was all over.

"Look at me, Regent Maximus!" I shouted.

Regent Maximus tossed up his head in his hurry to look, nearly throwing Mr. Henshaw off, but he managed a brief eye contact.

It steadied him (and gave Mr. Henshaw a chance to settle himself back down more securely).

Regent Maximus crept on. He cleared the tallest jump and excelled at the pause table, though I suspected he was penalized for squeezing his eyes shut while he stood there. All that was left was a series of hoops he had to climb through. These had given Regent Maximus a lot of trouble in the practice ring. Mr. Henshaw edged Regent Maximus toward them.

"Circle of death!" Regent Maximus squealed as he jumped—no, not jumped, but sort of step-hopped?—through the first hoop.

"Oh, why! Why is there another?" he cried as he stepped through the second. Only one more, but this one had a tiny pool of water on the other side. We'd prepared for water obstacles, but not *with* the hoop obstacle. Regent Maximus approached the final hoop.

"No! No! There is a lake! An ocean! WATER CARRIES DEADLY PATHOGENS." He began to back up. Marisol grabbed my hand in suspense—if Regent Maximus bumped into the hoop behind him, he'd spook, and then who *knew* what would happen!

"We're okay, we're okay," I heard Mr. Henshaw muttering, though he sounded a little nervous. He sat up straighter, like he was going to urge Regent Maximus back toward the hoop—

Regent Maximus cried, "There are no signs indicating this water's depth! I will drown! I DON'T THINK I CAN SWIM WITHOUT A FLOATIE—"

Mr. Henshaw tugged the reins to the right and led Regent Maximus not toward the jump, but off to the side.

They were skipping it entirely! Why was Mr. Henshaw giving up?

"Wait! What does that mean?" I asked Marisol. Had Regent Maximus just lost?

"It's a refusal—he won't get credit for it, but it's not terrible. And they'll get more points than they would have if Mr. Henshaw had gotten thrown," Marisol said, nodding enthusiastically. "It was a good decision!"

Regent Maximus seemed to think so too as he scurried away from the hoop. "We live! We survive!"

The baby Unicorns cheered as the buzzer sounded, indicating Mr. Henshaw and Regent Maximus had completed their round. The room lit up with applause! They'd done it! Marisol and I jumped up and down, then gave everyone we could reach high fives.

Scores were read soon after. Fortnight came in first. Between what had happened to Duchess and Forever Sunshine and the many Unicorns who didn't perform well because they were too busy worrying about their tails, Regent Maximus was now in the top six.

I couldn't wipe the grin off my face.

My smile vanished, though, when I went to congratulate Mr. Henshaw and Regent Maximus. I had just reached the nursery when I heard voices. I froze. It was Mr. Henshaw and . . . I recognized that accent . . . Prince Temujin!

I leaned in close to the nursery gate and strained to hear the conversation over the baby Unicorns. They had created a celebration song for Regent Maximus and were singing it loudly to him as they ran about.

"Oh, who's the strongest fastest bestest tallest rainbowest that we know? Regent Maximus! He's the Maximus! He's the loudest boldest smartest—"

"What are you doing?" Callie said, startling me so badly I bonked my nose into the gate. She was wearing fresh red lipstick and had recurled her hair. "Are you *spying*?"

"No! I was just . . . uh. Spying," I admitted.

"On Mr. Henshaw? Has he confessed? Was I right? He's the one behind the tail cutting?" Callie's eyes gleamed.

"What? No!"

Callie cut me off with a glorious snort. "Well, in that case, move aside, hay breath. *I'm* going to talk to the prince." She brushed past me and into the nursery.

"Henshaw," she said flatly, then, "Your Majesty! Or is it Highness? Calliope B. Bartlett, sir."

"Er, hello, Miss Bartlett," Prince Temujin replied. "Now, Mr. Henshaw, as I was saying—"

Callie persisted. "You know, Prince Temujin, Your

Highness Majesty, I'm a *huge* fan of your mother's. Some people say we look alike."

There was silence, other than the baby Unicorn song, for a few moments.

"Right. Anyhow, Mr. Henshaw," Prince Temujin went on, "I'd really love to add Regent Maximus to my stable— the rainbow mane and tail combination is so very rare. I'm sure you're well aware that Galatolia is, unfortunately, not a wealthy country. I can't offer you a lot of money, but I can promise him an excellent home."

I couldn't believe it. After all this, Mr. Henshaw was talking to the prince about selling Regent Maximus?

But Mr. Henshaw didn't sound so sure. "I appreciate the offer, but like I said, I'll let you know after the third round of the Trident. I just haven't decided. I know he's not performing particularly well—"

"Which is why my offer, small as it may be, might be the best one you'll get," Prince Temujin cut in, sounding a little more firm.

Mr. Henshaw was quiet for a moment. "I know that. But it's not really about the money. I bought Regent Maximus for the pleasure of showing a Unicorn, not to make money. I'll think on it, though."

Think on it! That meant he still *might* sell Regent Maximus!

I stood there simmering and upset long after I heard the prince's departing footsteps. Then I finally couldn't take it anymore. I flung open the gate. I hadn't realized Mr. Henshaw was so close, though—the gate crashed into him and knocked him to the lavender bedding. He slid toward Regent Maximus, who, for all his bravery in the ring today, had gone right back to being his same old self.

"Oh! It's a ground attack! He's going for our *knee-caps*!" Regent Maximus screeched, clambering away.

"Ground attack!" the babies cried with him. To my amazement, they began to leap away after Regent Maximus, mimicking his movements exactly. All the Unicorns came to rest in the far corner, near the blanket nests, and watched Mr. Henshaw pick himself up.

"If I'd known I was going to be thrown again," Mr. Henshaw observed, "I wouldn't have taken off my helmet."

"Sorry, Mr. Henshaw," I said, but my voice was sort of flat. In the distance, I heard Callie's voice, still peppering the prince with questions.

Mr. Henshaw sighed. I could tell he'd figured out that I'd heard about selling Regent Maximus.

"Now, Pip, nothing's decided. But showing a Unicorn is a lot more work than I expected. Maybe Regent Maximus would be happier in Galatolia, with other Unicorns," Mr. Henshaw said.

"But you had such a good time with him today!" I argued.

Mr. Henshaw rubbed his elbow, which was still covered with dirt and slime from his trip through the water hazard. "I sure did. That's why I only said I'd think about it. Don't be upset, Pip. I know you work hard with him. And it's not over yet."

Above us, a male Blankbird projected a picture onto a female Blankbird: It was a picture of my frown. I didn't feel equal to words, so I just pointed up at it.

Mr. Henshaw said, "Aw, Pip! I would never do it secretly, you know that, right? Whatever I decide, I'll tell you first."

I kept pointing at my frown on the Blankbird.

"Come on, let's go find your aunt," Mr. Henshaw said. "Remember, we still have to make it through round three!"

CHAPTER 18

Heeeeeeeeyyyyyyyyyyyyyy, Part Four

Aunt Emma arranged for me to have dinner at Tomas's house so she could take Callie to her dance lessons. I wasn't too happy about it at first—the final round of the Trident was tomorrow, and it felt like I should be helping Regent Maximus prepare. *But* I had to eat, and I also had to admit that it was nice to get away from the showgrounds for a while.

Ms. Ramirez sat us all down at the table. She was a fluffy woman who always looked very close to giving people hugs, which meant I tried to keep my distance. I liked her. But I also liked side hugs only.

"Family discussion time," Ms. Ramirez said, pouring herself a glass of tea. "First topic of discussion: Samuel, you burned this rice. How much is stuck onto the bottom of my pot now?"

Samuel blinked at her. He was one of Tomas's older triplet brothers. Even though they looked very similar, it wasn't actually that hard to tell them apart. Mostly it was just hard to remember which name went to which triplet. The other two triplets guffawed.

"You soak that pot," Ms. Ramirez said. "I'm not scraping rice until my old age."

"Second topic of discussion," Mr. Ramirez said. "How was the show today? Have they caught that tail cutter yet?"

I shook my head. "The police came, though. They said they're going to have an officer drive by a lot of times overnight to keep any more from getting cut."

"I just don't understand why anyone would sabotage the show like that," Ms. Ramirez said.

"Ahem," Tomas said. "Third topic of discussion."

All heads turned to him with various forms of surprise. I guessed Tomas didn't normally introduce topics of discussion.

"Yes, Tomas?" Ms. Ramirez asked.

He stood so that he could reach into the backpack that he'd hung on the back of his chair. Removing a red folder, he placed it on the table in front of him.

"I would like to get a pet."

Now we were all looking at him in surprise.

"But your allergies," Mr. Ramirez said.

"A hypoallergenic pet," Tomas explained. He opened the folder to reveal handwritten lists and photocopied images and the corner of a show bulletin. "I would like to get a Rockshine."

Now *I* was staring at him.

"What is a Rock—What is that?" asked Ms. Ramirez.

"I prepared materials," Tomas said. He handed out five identical stapled packets to each of his siblings and his parents. "I didn't make one for you, Pip, because you already know all about them."

I was still staring at him.

His family read the pamphlets.

"Fourth topic of discussion," said Eric, one of the triplets. "These things are super brown and dumb-looking."

"Eric, you apologize at once!" said Mr. Ramirez. "*Dumb* is not a word we use in this house."

"Sorry," Eric said. "I'm sure it's a *genius* at math. Too bad no one wants a sheep that does math."

Tomas was unfazed. He pushed up his glasses and told his parents, "I would take care of it. They're low-energy, and they don't require a lot of space, so I could keep it in the backyard without messing up the grass."

"Fifth topic of discussion," said Jorges, the third triplet. He tapped the sheet. "These things weigh three hundred pounds."

Tomas's father rapidly paged through his pamphlet. "Wait, where does it say that? Do they really?"

"Only mature males!" Tomas protested. "The breeder at the show has ones that are only one hundred. Pip, tell them."

I didn't want to let him down, so I said, as nicely as I could, "Tomas is right—they're around one hundred each. They're actually one of the smallest varieties of magical livestock."

"We aren't zoned for livestock," Mr. Ramirez said. "The city and S.M.A.C.K.E.D. won't allow it."

"No, no," Tomas insisted. "I looked up the codes." He was still completely unflustered—I was so amazed! He never stuck up for himself like this. "Three breeds of Rockshine are allowed inside Cloverton city limits, and that's the kind I want. And you see on page four, turn the page—yes, that page. See, right there. And they are very hardy and live on regular hay, just one flake every three days."

His parents frowned at the pages. I leaned closer to Jorges so I could see what Tomas had given them.

"And if you turn to page seven," Tomas continued, "I prepared a financial report so you can see how my weekly allowance would cover the food and initial vaccinations so I'd only need your help if an emergency happened."

His parents made muttering noises. Ms. Ramirez ate some more rice. Sam offered me a fruit plate.

"What is this last page?" Mr. Ramirez asked finally.

Tomas said, "When I told Ms. Gould what I was doing, she suggested I put that page in."

I leaned over to look at it. It was a picture of Tomas and one of the Rockshines, clearly snapped at the Trident.

"This is pretty touching," Eric said.

Tomas ignored this. To his parents, he said, "And I would use the money I was saving up for a new humidifier for my room to get one from Ms. Gould."

"Obviously, we're going to have to think about it," Ms. Ramirez said. She held up the papers. "Can we keep this?"

"Those are yours to take with you," Tomas said solemnly.

"Maybe we'll talk to this Ms. Gould person," Mr. Ramirez said. "And your aunt, Pip. Do you have any thoughts to add?"

I was pretty impressed by all the work Tomas had put into his presentation. I mean, I still didn't like Rockshines all that much, but then, some people didn't like magical creatures, or marshmallows, or books all that much. So I shrugged and said, "I bet Tomas would make a really good Rockshine owner."

Tomas beamed at me.

Later, the two of us sat in the backyard as I smacked mosquitoes and he drew another map. He was labeling places where the fence might need to be reinforced for a

Rockshine. I doodled animals on the heel of my hand with a pen and thought about how Mr. Henshaw was considering selling Regent Maximus.

Finally, I asked, "What do you think about what Callie says? About Mr. Henshaw being the person cutting the tails off?"

Tomas sighed heavily. "I dunno. I like him, but . . ." He tapped his pencil on the paper. "It helps him out, doesn't it? He had Regent Maximus for sale from the start of the show, and now that he's doing better, people are asking about buying him . . ."

I guess I had thought Tomas would say Callie was being silly. But maybe he had a point. Maybe *Callie* had a point. I thought back to the night of the emergency visit to the Rockshines, trying to sort out if the shadowy figure near Duchess's stall was Mr. Henshaw. The person looked about Mr. Henshaw's height. And I remembered how the policewoman said they weren't able to get in touch with Mr. Henshaw.

Was that because he was too busy running away with a Unicorn tail to answer his phone?

"I don't know," I said reluctantly. "I wish there was a way to prove it one way or the other."

Tomas shrugged. "Just keep an eye on him before the Trident tomorrow, maybe."

I nodded. "Can you help, or will you be with the Rockshines?"

He looked at me witheringly. "Come on, Pip. I wouldn't miss Regent Maximus's final round for all the Rockshines in the world!"

CHAPTER 19

Sometimes Popcorn Is a Crime-Solving Food

Even if I hadn't known it was the final round of the Triple Trident, I would have figured it out the minute I stepped onto the showgrounds the next morning. An additional huge yellow banner had been hung over the main double doors to enter the area. TRIDENT ROUND, it read. As soon as we stepped inside, a girl wearing a Triple Trident shirt handed me a brand-new show bulletin for the day.

Just looking at it made me feel nervous for Regent Maximus, even without being worried about Mr. Henshaw and the Unicorn tails. Tomas and I had stayed up late making shirts for ourselves, Aunt Emma, and Callie that said TEAM REGENT MAXIMUS on them. Tomas had a second shirt that said ROCKSHINES RULE underneath his—so he could pull the top shirt off and wear the second for the Rockshine Special Show later that day. (He'd offered to make me one too, but I said no thanks.)

It felt like everyone at the entire show had come to

watch the final round. Vendors sold snacks and drinks by the seating area entrance. I saw the two police officers standing near the entrance, watching people carefully. Like Tomas had said: If the Unicorn tail cutter were to strike again, it'd have to be today.

Aunt Emma, Tomas, Callie, and I found seats at the very top of the bleachers. Marisol and one of her sisters were nearby. I waved.

"That's your friend from EverSun, right?" Aunt Emma asked. "I hope their Unicorn does well. I feel so bad for them, that the other had her tail cut."

"Me too," I said, and wondered again about Mr. Henshaw. Tomas met my eyes, and I could tell he was thinking the same thing.

The crowd suddenly hushed. All eyes went to the judges' podium. The announcer was standing up, and even from this far away, I could see his eyes glinting with excitement.

"Ladies and gentlemen!" he said, voice booming. "The final round of the Triple Trident will now begin!"

When I saw the first five beautiful Unicorn finalists mincing around the ring, their manes and tails streaming, it suddenly reminded me of just how excited I'd been to come to this show in the first place. They were so glorious that I felt a sudden urge to leap up and down, or squeeze my hands into fists, or draw a picture of the moment in my *Guide*. Instead, I furiously traced a Unicorn head on my arm with my finger, over and over again, grinning.

The judges were just now walking to their seats, and I saw they were all wearing their fanciest clothes—Prince Temujin, who came out last, was even wearing a tuxedo.

"Go Fortnight!" Marisol cheered.

Tomas echoed, "Go Fo—" but then a blue bubble came out of his mouth. He dug in his pocket for his allergy medicine.

The sixth Unicorn was Regent Maximus. He wasn't really mincing like the others. It was more . . . power walking. Still, he looked pretty great. His rainbow mane and tail stood out among the other Unicorns, who all had solid-colored hair. I couldn't help but notice how our training had paid off. Just a few days before, he'd had to stare at me the entire time while slinking through the ring on his belly. Now he was able to move with just a quick glance to me or to Mr. Henshaw. Practice really did make perfect! Or, well, partly perfect.

"Ladies and gentlemen, for the final round of the Triple Trident, please welcome your Miss Triple Trident Tiara!" the announcer said. Behind the Unicorns came a girl wearing an enormously flouffy blue ball gown. She had a tiara that was at least a foot tall and was wearing a white sash that read MISS TRIPLE TRIDENT TIARA in big black letters.

Because we didn't have real royalty in Cloverton, the pageant queen would be the "princess" for the final round of the Trident. Each Unicorn had to lay its head gently on the princess's lap, just like Unicorns in storybooks did. Unicorns would be judged on how beautifully and picturesquely they did so. I thought that even if Regent Maximus didn't look particularly graceful, his bright white horn and rainbow mane would probably look pretty against the princess's dress—

"Uh-oh," Tomas said.

He had just had the same thought I had. I said, grimly, *"Blue."*

We hadn't planned on Regent Maximus being faced with the color he was most afraid of.

But there was nothing to be done about it now.

One by one, the Unicorns trotted up to Miss Triple Trident Tiara and sank into dramatic and elegant poses to lay their heads down in her lap. The girl looked a bit nervous about it—who wouldn't be alarmed by a three-foot-long Unicorn horn waving so close to her eyes?—but she pulled a smile out of somewhere and waved to the cameras that flashed wildly each time a Unicorn settled into its final pose.

It really did look like something out of a storybook!

Then it was Regent Maximus's turn.

"Blue! Blue! Why does it follow me everywhere?" he wailed as Mr. Henshaw led him toward the makeshift princess. "It's always watching me from above! And now! Blue! I LOOK AT THE BLUE AND FIND IT IS LOOKING BACK!"

A murmur of worry went through the crowd. Regent Maximus would never mean to hurt anyone, of course, but the horn on his head was gleaming and sharp. If he got scared and jerked away, things could go bad really fast.

"You can do it, Regent Maximus!" someone cheered.

It was *Callie*. I turned around and stared at her with surprise. But then Aunt Emma cheered too, and then Tomas, and Marisol, and the other Barreras, and me. Soon everyone in the entire ring was shouting for Regent Maximus! All the way from the top of the bleachers, I could see Mr. Henshaw blush.

Regent Maximus couldn't understand everyone else, but I saw him look toward me with big watery eyes.

"You've got this!" I shouted. "Remember—the babies are watching!"

More than anything else, *this* seemed to give Regent Maximus courage. He straightened just a bit, marching forward, and then slowly, slowly, slowly lowered his head onto Miss Triple Trident Tiara's lap. He looked a little less noble and more like he might be sick to his stomach.

But the crowd went wild anyway.

He was not yet Jeffrey Higgleston's Ideal Unicorn. But he was a lot closer than when we'd begun.

The cheering went on and on.

The judges nodded to the crowd, satisfied that they had all the information they needed, and walked back up to the booth to start figuring out the overall winner.

There was nothing to do but wait! I leaned against the back of the bleachers and tried not to hold my breath in anticipation. Marisol hurried over to her family to wait for the results, while Aunt Emma started talking to some other grown-ups about the pink stripes in her hair. A couple of Blankbirds were also chatting away just overhead.

"I'll tell you one thing: I'll be glad when this contest is over," the male said.

"Oh? Why's that?"

"Because look at all that popcorn," the male Blankbird said, projecting an image of one of the Trident's many popcorn stalls onto the female. "You know these humans can't eat it all. They'll throw it away."

"We'll feast!" the female said excitedly. "Popcorn dance!"

"Exactly," the male said, sounding pleased.

I laughed—I liked the idea of the Blankbirds throwing another big dance party the night that the show was done. Apparently, the Blankbirds did too, because the male continued to project images of different popcorn stalls onto the female.

"Wait!" I gasped, so suddenly that the birds started. "Don't fly away, please!"

The birds peered at me and then at one another.

Standing up, I leaned over the back railing of the bleachers, waving as the Blankbirds cocked their heads to one side and then, as a pair, cocked them to the other side.

"Is she talking to us?" the male asked.

"Yes! I have a question. You know about the Unicorns getting their tails cut off?" I called.

The female Blankbird hopped up and down a bit. "Unicorns? Tails cut off? When?"

"A few nights ago, a purple Unicorn named Duchess. And before that, an orange one named Forever Sunshine—"

"Oh! I seem to remember. You were here that one night!" the female Blankbird said, then leaned toward the male to whisper, "She caught Alexandra and Joseph hosting their dance party, didn't you hear?"

"Yes! That night!" I said.

"I remember it. We didn't go to the dance party, because someone had left a bag of cheese puffs on the ground," the male said.

"Those were delicious," the female added.

"Yes, yes, I'm sure they were." I tried to contain my hopefulness. "Did you by any chance get a look at *who* cut the Unicorn tails off? And can you show me, if you did?"

"Hm. I think . . ." The male Blankbird projected images from that night onto the female.

The Blankbirds were clearly more focused on food than on a Unicorn show scandal. The male Blankbird continued to flicker through images, while the female commented on how delicious all the food had been—

"Wait! Go back!" I yelled. Tomas heard me and climbed over a lower bleacher to join me. It didn't take him long to sort out what was happening. The male Blankbird went back to a shot of a box of gummy bears lying sideways on the ground. The ground around them was littered in lavender—

It was the Unicorn hall!

"Can you get closer?" Tomas asked the Blankbird. I translated so the Blankbird could understand.

"Let's see—Oh! I have a flyover shot!" The Blankbird changed the image to a shot from overhead. The box of gummy bears was a speck on the floor of the Unicorn hall. The backs of the Unicorns were glossy and bright, their horns little circles from this angle.

"This is too early. Duchess still has her tail," Tomas pointed to Duchess's swishy, thick, silvery tail. The Blankbird continued to show us shots as he flew down to the box of gummy bears. When Duchess went out of view entirely, she still had her tail.

"Oh," I said, disappointed. "I thought maybe you'd have a shot of the tail cutter."

"We were really just very excited about the gummy bears," the female Blankbird said apologetically, fluffing her feathers so that the image went blurry. When she settled, I noticed something—

A person!

Well, a *shadow*. In the very last image, in the far left corner, just before the Blankbirds landed on the gummy bears, there was a shadow. I pointed and yelped for the Blankbirds to stay still so I could get a good look. It was definitely a person, and he was definitely dressed all in black, just like the man I'd caught a glimpse of that night. This had to be him!

"It's awfully blurry," Tomas said warily.

"And he's not even facing the camera—I mean, the Blankbird," I added.

"But at least now you know it's a man with a bald spot," Tomas said, trying to help.

I blinked at him. "What?"

Tomas pointed to the center of the female Blankbird's chest. "Right there. That's a bald spot, right?"

I narrowed my eyes—I'd thought it was just a trick of the light! But no, Tomas was right. Just in the center of the man's head, a pale patch of skin curved so that it looked a little like a heart.

A heart!

My eyes went wide. I looked at the Blankbirds, then Tomas, then back to the image.

No! I thought. *It couldn't be!*

"Pip! What's going on?" Tomas asked.

"I know someone who has a bald spot just like that—in the shape of a heart!" I said, whispering with panic.

"Who?"

I turned and pointed hard at the judges' booth. "Prince Temujin!"

Toupee or Not Toupee— That Is the Question!

"Ladies and gentlemen! We're ready to announce the winner of the Thirty-Fourth Annual Triple Trident!" The announcer's voice sprang up over the loudspeaker, the papers he held crumpling as he arranged them with his microphone.

Tomas and I jerked our heads over to look at the judges' table. The judges, including Prince Temujin and his toupee, had returned to the table with their results.

"We've got to tell Aunt Emma before the judges leave," I told Tomas urgently. "That the Blankbirds can prove it was the prince. Because that bald spot there—"

I spun around to show him again . . . but the Blankbirds I'd just been talking with were gone! With a groan, I searched the immediate area for them. There were two Blankbirds near the trash can, and another two near the churro stall, and another two in the rafters. It was impossible to tell which ones I'd just spoken with! There went my proof!

"Tomas, come on!"

He didn't know my plan, but he followed me without question. I might not have been able to show Aunt Emma the Blankbirds, but I could at least tell the police who to investigate. They had the Wimpelings, after all, and they'd certainly be able to match the scent from Duchess's stall to Prince Temujin.

Tomas and I trundled down the steps. It was impossible to go quietly. Not only was everyone else sitting, but they were also all *quiet*. The banging of our steps down the bleachers sounded like metal explosions. People stared—the *judges* stared.

Without meaning to, my eyes locked on Prince Temujin's.

I saw him swallow.

And I was certain he *knew* why I was racing down the bleachers. Or at least, he knew something was up.

"In second place, the winner of the silver trident . . . Morgana's Green with Envy!" the announcer said. The crowd cheered, and a tall green Unicorn with a wispy white tail pranced forward. The judges—including Prince Temujin—helped lower a wreath of sunflowers around the Unicorn's neck while the handler lifted a silver Trident high above his head.

"Where are the police officers?" I asked Tomas. We

were on ground level now, and I suddenly didn't see uniforms anywhere.

"And in third place, the winner of the bronze trident . . . Callaloo's Multicolored Lies the Head That Wears the Crown!" the announcer said. The crowd went wild.

"Whoa!" Tomas and I both said at the same time, realizing what had just happened.

Regent Maximus had won third place!

I looked back into the arena. They were already announcing the first-place winner—Fortnight—which meant most of the applause and confetti and celebrating was for him, not Regent Maximus. But I didn't care! The judges handed Mr. Henshaw a bronze trident. They tried to put a wreath of pink peonies around Regent Maximus's neck, but he scrambled away (over the crowd, I heard him shout something about the potential for bee infestation).

"He got third! He didn't get last place!" I said, amazed. Then I shouted, "Way to go, Regent Maximus!" The Unicorn looked over at me; I gave him a big thumbs-up sign. I could barely see Mr. Henshaw's face because the judge had handed him the peony wreath, but in between all the pink flower petals, I could see he was still blushing with happiness. A judge went to shake his hand—

Prince Temujin!

"Oh, right. Let's go!" I said, shaking off the excitement. We could celebrate with Regent Maximus later! I still didn't see police officers anywhere. I jogged into the ring toward the prince. Trouble was, the crowd was spilling down into the ring. Everyone wanted to congratulate the winners, and the way forward was a sea of elbows and knees and children and adults and Unicorns.

"There! He's right there!" I said, jumping up and down to point. As if on cue, Prince Temujin looked over his shoulder and saw me in the crowd. His eyes widened, and I saw him turn back to Mr. Henshaw.

Even from here, I heard him. He was speaking in a quick, clipped voice. A guilty voice. A nervous voice. He was going to run for it. "Well, great show! Nice meeting you! I've got to be going. Yes, yes. I have a plane to catch! We'll be in touch!"

He began to wind his way through the crowd. I could tell he was trying to go fast but also look casual about it. I didn't care about looking casual, but I did care about being fast. Too bad that with all the grown-ups and Unicorns and vendors and *people* that were bigger than me, I could barely move! I finally pushed through to the other side of the ring, just in time to see Prince Temujin break into a jog. He was weaving between Llamadors, running for the exit!

But just when he was about to fly through the doors, the police officers finally walked in. They had their hands in their pockets and looked almost bored. They clearly didn't *mean* to show up just then. Still, Prince Temujin was spooked. He took a sharp turn and hurried off to the left, toward the Glimmerbeast pens.

Go go go! I chanted to myself as Tomas and I ran along behind him. The Glimmerbeast area was full of pens and paddocks and booths—it'd be so easy for him to lose us in there!

"I've got an idea!" I heard Tomas shout behind me. I looked back at him; he was trying to explain the idea, but had to stop in order to puff on his inhaler as we ran.

"Just do it! Whatever it is, do it!" I shouted back, because I had basically *zero* ideas at the moment. I ducked under a display of Pegasus saddles—Prince Temujin was a few hundred feet ahead. He was running now, so desperate to get away he didn't even care that people were staring. I nearly crashed into a lady leading a Manticore—

"Hey!" the lady said.

"Hey!" the Manticore said, and blasted me with some steam.

"Sorry! Excuse me, sorry!" I said, holding out my hands and charging on. Prince Temujin's tuxedo tails were flapping behind him, but he was getting farther and farther ahead. He cut to the right, and we raced parallel to each other along the Glimmerbeast pens. There was an exit up ahead! Prince Temujin vaulted over a fence, losing his bow tie in the process. He was going to cross through the pen and get to the door!

Wait—no. Someone was standing in front of it!

Tomas was standing in front of it. He had his inhaler in one hand and shook it, the little metallic clink making it all the way to my ears. Prince Temujin slowed to a stop and put his hands on his knees in the middle of the pen, then glanced back at me. He was trapped—and he had to go through me or go through Tomas to get out. Sweat was running down his face, and his mouth was open, gasping for breath.

"I know it was you, Prince Temujin! And even if you get out, I'm going to tell everyone!" I shouted.

The prince laughed—well, he *tried* to laugh, but he was out of breath, so he mostly just wheezed. "Even *if* they believe you, Pip, I'll be halfway home to Galatolia by then."

He turned and sprinted straight at Tomas.

I held my breath. Tomas squeezed his eyes shut and balled his hands into fists at his sides, like rather than fighting Prince Temujin, he was just going to transform into a brick wall.

"Move, Tomas!" I shouted, because as much as I

wanted Prince Temujin to be stopped, I didn't want to see my best friend get smushed.

Tomas didn't move.

He whistled.

I didn't know Tomas knew how to whistle, for starters, so I was pretty impressed. But when I realized what he was whistling for, I was *really* impressed.

The prince—who was just a few seconds from knocking Tomas to the ground and busting out the door—suddenly yelped. He tripped over nothing whatsoever, flew through the air, and then he was . . . flying?

No! Not flying! Tomas whistled again, sharper this time, and patted his knees. There was a commotion of hooves and brays from the seemingly empty pen. The prince wasn't flying—he was being bustled along on the backs of stampeding invisible Rockshines! Tomas jogged back and forth, and the Rockshines seemed to follow him—I could tell because Prince Temujin was shouting and clinging on to invisible hair, waving back and forth behind Tomas like a kite tail.

There were footsteps behind me—the police officers'. Together, we watched Prince Temujin bumbling along through thin air.

"Bring him this way, Tomas!" I called.

"Is he a wizard?" the police officers asked.

I shook my head. "No. Just a Rockshine specialist."

Tomas took a big, wide circle to me, then abruptly sat down. The Rockshines wheeled to a stop; Prince Temujin slid to the ground, his fancy clothes covered in dust and straw and his toupee fluttering open like the flap of an envelope.

The police officers didn't even ask questions. They just faced me and waited for answers.

"Prince Temujin. He's the one who cut off the Unicorn tails!" I said.

"The Rockshines stopped him from escaping the country," Tomas added proudly. The Rockshines had gathered around him and were blinking on and off into visibility, like Christmas lights—if Christmas lights were brownish gray. Or grayish brown.

"Hey!" one of the Rockshines said accusingly to Prince Temujin. The prince flinched at the noise.

The first police officer—her name tag said that her name was McDonald—asked, "How do you know the prince stole the tails?"

I explained about the Blankbirds, and then about how I'd lost the pair of them that I'd seen project the image of the prince's bald spot. We all gazed up at the rafters; there were many Blankbirds watching us.

"Well, that's okay. We'll just get the Wimpeling!" McDonald said.

"The *what*?" Prince Temujin was trying to sound official and professional and princelike, but it was hard to take him seriously since there was a big Rockshine footprint in the middle of his forehead.

"We used Wimpelings to analyze smells from the Unicorn pens. Just a quick formality. Once you've been cleared, you'll be free to go," the other officer said, patting Prince Temujin on the shoulder. It was pretty clear that he didn't think the prince was responsible. McDonald, however, didn't seem so sure. She lifted her radio to her mouth and called for another officer to bring a Wimpeling to the Rockshine stalls.

"Good, yes," the prince said, but I could tell he was nervous—the Wimpeling would prove I was telling the truth. He cleared his throat and went on, "And what about these two? They tried to crush me with these . . . sheep . . . things."

"Rockshines," I corrected.

"The most common variety of Glimmerbeasts," Tomas added.

"And Rockshines are really quite harmless, Your Majesty," McDonald said, and smiled at him. The prince didn't smile back. He looked longingly at the door he'd nearly escaped through.

Finally, another police officer came rushing up with the big orange bucket I knew housed a Wimpeling. Behind him was a small crowd—people from the Unicorn show, mostly, some of whom were still leading their Unicorns.

"Sorry," the new police officer—his name tag said his last name was Krogh—said. "They overheard you on the radio."

"Wait, the prince? Or Pip? *What's going on?*" someone—Mr. Barrera, who was leading Fortnight behind him—said. Marisol was beside him, her eyes wide. Aunt Emma and Callie pushed their way to the front, and I saw Regent Maximus and Mr. Henshaw peering through the crowd from the back.

"Pip! What did you *do* to the prince?" Callie asked, tidying her hair and smiling at Prince Temujin as she spoke.

"Pip! They tried to put *flowers on my head*," Regent Maximus cried.

I ignored them—I was too busy watching the police officer with the Wimpeling. Prince Temujin shifted a little as the bucket neared him. Tomas left the Rockshines to stand beside me.

"So a Wimpeling is some sort of . . . um . . ." Prince Temujin said, trying to spy into the bucket.

"It's a variety of magical sea slug," I said.

McDonald reached into the bucket to pull out the soggy Wimpeling. The crowd made a loud "ew" noise; Fortnight gagged. McDonald and I both glared at them.

The other officer smiled a little at the prince. "We'll just need to let it get a good smell of you."

"You're going to put that thing *on me*?" the prince asked, horrified.

"Oh, it doesn't bite, and it's not slime season," McDonald reassured him. "It'd be best if we put it on your face. There's no way it can get a face scent wrong."

"*My face?*" Prince Temujin looked at me, then Tomas, then the Wimpeling. I put my hands on my hips. A little Wimpeling to the face was nothing compared to the Unicorns losing their tails!

"All right, close your eyes," McDonald said, walking up.

The Wimpeling quivered, and I heard it say, "Oh yes! Delicious smells! Let me at them!"

McDonald lifted the Wimpeling. "One, two—"

Prince Temujin held up his palms. "No! I did it!"

"What?" Mr. Barrera shouted.

The prince put his head in his hands and shouted, "I cut the Unicorn tails!"

CHAPTER 21

Someday My Prince Will Come . . . to Jail

The crowd gasped. The police officers gasped. Even Tomas gasped—wait, no, he was just using his inhaler.

The crowd began shouting angrily as they recovered from their shock.

"Ruiner!"

"Traitor!"

"Sabotage!"

"I wasn't trying to sabotage anything!" the prince said pleadingly, looking for—and not finding—sympathetic eyes. "I was trying to *save* something."

"What do you mean?" Krogh demanded.

The prince took a deep breath and looked over the settling crowd. "My country—Galatolia—is very proud of our magical creatures. We once had more unique magical creatures in our borders than anywhere else in the world. Some scientists even think Galatolia had Dragons once! But over time, so many have been lost. The Galatolia

Galloper and the Sherrybill have already gone extinct. The Junebird, our national symbol, is endangered."

"What's a Junebird?" Mr. Barrera asked. He didn't sound very touched by the prince's story so far, and I couldn't really blame him.

I spoke up. "It's a very rare magical bird. They lay golden eggs and have long tails."

"They're extraordinary," the prince said fondly. "And they're almost gone. You see, they lay only a single egg every few years. Because the eggs are golden, thieves steal them from the nests. Now, Galatolia is down to only a handful of Junebirds, and we're doing everything we can to keep them safe."

"What does that have to do with Unicorn tails?" someone asked impatiently.

The prince took another big breath. "Junebirds only build their nests from Unicorn tails. The finer the quality of the tail, the more likely the Junebird will love the nest and lay her egg there. We have Unicorns in Galatolia, of course, but they're smaller, rougher varieties—whereas the Triple Trident hosts Unicorns with the finest tails in the world."

"But why steal them?" Marisol asked, sounding hurt. "You ruined Duchess's chances! You could have at least waited till after the show!"

Junebird

The Junebird's beak is designed for extracting the juice from rosy nectarines

The color of the feathers is usually the same as the color of the Unicorn-hair nest it was hatched in

The Junebird would rather run than fly, as its wings are not generally strong enough to lift its massive tail for long

Junebirds are one of three magical creatures that are attracted to emotion. The gentle Junebird is strangely drawn to anger, and flocks of Junebirds can often be found watching human arguments

SIZE: 36-40"
WEIGHT: 11-14 lbs.
DESCRIPTION: The beautiful Junebird is the symbol of Galatolia, where it once flourished. It is now endangered due to habitat destruction, a shortage of rosy nectarines, and the rarity of quality Unicorn tails, as Junebirds will only build their nests with Unicorn-tail hairs.

The prince shook his head mournfully. "If Junebirds can't make a nest of quality, they simply *don't*, and it'll be another few years before they try again. Three of our breeding pairs have started looking for Unicorn tails, and, of course, haven't found any. I *have* to get back to Galatolia with the Unicorn tails. The survival of the species is at stake! I cut only two tails—that already means that one of our pairs won't be able to have an egg this time around."

I had to admit, this changed things. Of *course* it wasn't right for the prince to cut off Unicorns' tails. But I also knew it wasn't right for a whole species to go extinct. I wanted to say something, but didn't know how to tell the crowd how I felt. Luckily, Aunt Emma stepped up.

"The survival of a species is very, very important, Prince Temujin. I know we all agree with that," she said, and the other grown-ups nodded. "But these are very expensive show Unicorns—"

"We don't have the money to buy them!" Prince Temujin interrupted.

Aunt Emma held up a calm hand and, when the prince quieted, went on, "It will be a long while before Duchess and Forever Sunshine can show again. Not to mention the time and money all the people who pulled out of the competition wasted."

The crowd nodded again, a little more ferociously this time.

"*But* . . . what's done is done. So while I'm sure you'll have to go with these police officers to see about the consequences of your crime, I'll see to it that the Unicorn tails you've already cut are sent to Galatolia and given to the Junebirds. That is, if EverSun Unicorns and Forever Sparkle Stables are all right with that?" she said, looking over to the Barreras and the man who owned Forever Sunshine.

Mr. Barrera put a hand on Marisol's shoulder; she looked up at him and nodded. "Of course. It's already done, so I'm happy to help the Junebirds."

"Same here," the other man said with a stiff lip.

Prince Temujin breathed a huge sigh of relief. He didn't look happy, exactly—he was still about to get arrested, after all—but he looked like he was glad it was all over. McDonald and Krogh each put a hand on his shoulders and led him away from the Rockshines, who were now busily licking Tomas's shoes.

"Hey," one said adoringly.

Tomas reached down to pat its head. "Oh. Their eyes need to be wiped," he said happily, then pulled out a tissue.

Aunt Emma and Callie made their way toward me,

followed by Regent Maximus and Mr. Henshaw. It really said something about how boring the Rockshines were that Regent Maximus wasn't afraid of them. While the grown-ups talked, I explained to Regent Maximus what had just happened.

"A *bird*? Birds are going to steal my tail?" Regent Maximus said, eyes wide.

"No, no—first of all, those birds are far away. And secondly, the prince is gone, so he can't steal your tail. Don't worry, Regent Maximus. Your show career is just starting!"

This *did* worry Regent Maximus. He sucked in his lips and pawed at the ground. "I got third place, you know."

"I do know! I'm so proud of you," I said.

"But I still have to do more shows?" he asked, voice lowered to a whisper.

I sighed. "Come on, Regent Maximus. You did a great job! And Mr. Henshaw really had a good time too. Didn't you have a *little* fun?"

Regent Maximus looked warily at a woman in a large hat walking by, like he thought the brim might take a bite out of him.

"Well," he said, "I did think training for the show was fun. And I liked the baby Unicorns and our disaster preparations, because I think it's good that they know about how the world is scary. And I liked my stall, with the picture you drew."

"But not the show? Not at all?" I asked, a little disappointed. I guessed I'd figured that once Regent Maximus could make it through a show, he'd learn to love it. But the Unicorn just shook his head quickly.

"Is there a way I can do the shows, but never have to leave the baby Unicorn pen?" he asked, sounding hopeful.

"Afraid not," I said, frowning. But it didn't seem very fair that Regent Maximus should *still* have to be a show Unicorn. He'd given it a fair try, after all. I licked my lips, then walked over to where Mr. Henshaw and Aunt Emma were talking.

Mr. Henshaw grinned. "Pip! Third place! I would really like for you to have the Trident. *You* earned it, after all, training him."

"Oh! Thanks! I've never gotten a trophy in anything before," I said. "But . . . um . . . Mr. Henshaw? There's something I wanted to ask you."

"Of course," Mr. Henshaw said, frowning. "Is something wrong?"

"It's just that . . . I don't think Regent Maximus really liked showing very much. I think he liked getting to know *you* better, and I know he liked being in the pen with the baby Unicorns, but I'm just not sure showing is for him."

Mr. Henshaw nodded but didn't look like this was good news. I panicked, and added, "I'm sure if it was between showing and being sold, he'd—"

"No, no, calm down, Pip," Mr. Henshaw said, smiling a little. "The truth is, I didn't love showing either. Pretty dumb of me to buy an expensive show Unicorn before I figured that out, huh?"

"Yep," Aunt Emma said before I could answer, and Mr. Henshaw laughed.

"But I *did* like getting to know Regent Maximus better. He's a pretty great Unicorn, even if he is a little scared. That's what makes him so brave—he tries hard even when he's frightened. It's pretty admirable. I think he'll love being a pet Unicorn."

"So does that mean you're keeping him? He'll be *your* pet Unicorn?" I asked.

"Of course!" Mr. Henshaw said, walking over to pat Regent Maximus on the nose. "Plenty of people have expensive dogs as pets. Why not an expensive Unicorn? I've grown pretty attached to him."

I grinned. "Hey! In that case . . ." I took a step closer so I could be certain Regent Maximus would hear what I was about to suggest. "What if Regent Maximus donated his tail to the Junebirds?"

"Oh!" Aunt Emma and Mr. Henshaw said at once. They glanced at each other.

"It *would* help save an endangered species," Aunt Emma said.

"And I think he might actually like a shorter tail. Sometimes I think he's afraid of it?" Mr. Henshaw said.

I lifted my eyebrows. "Afraid of his own tail?"

Regent Maximus interrupted to whisper, "It's *always chasing me*. So yes! I'll donate it! Who wants it? They can have it!"

I waved Marisol over, and she plaited Regent Maximus's tail into a long, thick braid. Aunt Emma borrowed some shears from Ms. Gould's Rockshine grooming kit and carefully cut Regent Maximus's tail. It *was* a beautiful tail—it looked like Aunt Emma was holding a rainbow in her hand.

"I'm free!" Regent Maximus said, waving the little stump that remained back and forth. The other Unicorn owners looked a bit horrified by what we'd done, but Regent Maximus pranced his feet, pleased with himself. Mr. Henshaw laughed and offered him a handful of honeycomb—broken into very tiny pieces—as a reward.

"Hurry, Pip. Go catch the prince and find out what we

need to do in order to get this to Galatolia!" Aunt Emma said, handing the tail to me.

I nodded and took off in the direction of the prince and the police officers—they were just slipping out the front door!

"Wait! Prince Temujin, wait!" I shouted, waving my arms in the air. "We have a third Unicorn tail! It's being donated! We just need to know where to send it—"

The prince spun around upon hearing this, face erupting into a happy grin. Unfortunately, doing so unbalanced Krogh and McDonald, who'd been walking closely beside him. Krogh lost his footing and reached out for balance. His hand hit the edge of the Wimpeling bucket McDonald was holding, sending it swinging up, up, up . . .

Until the Wimpeling came sliding out. I held my breath as it tipped off the bucket's edge. McDonald shouted. The prince looked up. His eyes went wide. His mouth went round.

He yelled, "Oh no—"

That was all he had time to yell. The Wimpeling slapped down on his face with a tremendous *SPLAT*, tendrils of slime still slicing through the air.

"Delicious smells!" the Wimpeling nickered joyously, then begin making a little trilling noise—the noise that indicated it had just matched scents.

CHAPTER 22

The Ideal Unicorn (and the Ideal Rockshine)

I think if I were writing a book on training Unicorns, I'd probably include some stuff even Jeffrey Higgleston himself wouldn't think to put in. *Pip Bartlett's Guide to Unicorn Training* would include notes about Unicorn personalities, for instance. Because even though Jeffrey Higgleston was right about some Unicorns being proud and brave, like Fortnight, not *all* Unicorns are like that. And even though he wrote that Unicorns are "the most beautiful of the magical creatures" and the most ideally suited to being shown for sport, not all Unicorns are happy in the show ring.

Also, everything looks more organized on paper. I think I'd try to write more about the hard work behind the show scenes. When I daydreamed about the Triple Trident, I knew about the three days of beautiful Unicorns prancing around and showing their stuff, but I never thought about how the people who showed them spent all of the other days of the year doing exactly the sorts of chores I did at the Cloverton Clinic. Shoveling poop. Feeding. It makes it a little less magical, I guess, to know how much practical work there is in it. Less magical, but more impressive.

On the last day of the Trident, Marisol and I exchanged e-mail addresses and phone numbers and promised to be better friends when school started again. Regent Maximus wished the Unicorn babies a tearful good-bye ("I'll miss you! Remember to never step in puddles, because you could get Blandworms! Never look into the sun or you'll go blind!"), and I promised him that I'd come visit him at Mr. Henshaw's soon. Aunt Emma kept in touch with Officer McDonald about the Junebirds, and just a few short days after the Triple Trident, Aunt Emma triumphantly displayed a printed-out e-mail from an official Galatolia address.

"The first pair of Junebirds laid an egg already!" she said excitedly.

I also got an e-mail from Marisol. She'd just signed up for a therapy-animal session with Duchess! They were training to visit hospitals so that people could admire a Unicorn and feel better. Marisol said that it was actually

Pip Bartlett's Guide to the Ideal Unicorn

The ideal Unicorn is a thing of joy and
wonder, a marvelous combination of elegance
and performance that is unmatched in the
animal kingdom. Unicorns, like the humans who
admire them, come in all different kinds.
Some are brave, some are protective, some are
gentle, some are wise. The things that some
Unicorns are suited to will be terrible chores
for others; you just can't tell until you
spend some time with that particular speciman.
The ideal Unicorn is a happy Unicorn.

lucky Duchess had no tail, because it was less likely to get caught in the automatic doors in hospital buildings. So she was getting a happy ending after all.

That left Tomas and his Rockshine.

His parents decided that he couldn't have a Rockshine in their backyard, because it would completely ruin the backyard for gardening and playing . . . but they said he could have one if it could live in Mr. Henshaw's stable with Regent Maximus!

Tomas was out of his mind with excitement.

I couldn't believe he hadn't lost interest, but here we were, just a few days after the Triple Trident, waiting at Mr. Henshaw's stable for Mariah Gould's Rockshine trailer to pull up on its way out of town.

Mr. Henshaw, Aunt Emma, and I stood in the full sun with Tomas's parents. We all watched the road impatiently. Tomas was inside the stable, going through a twelve-step checklist of tasks he intended to complete to make the space comfortable and safe for his Rockshine.

Regent Maximus watched from his stall, his head stretched over the door and his big eyes on the road too. He asked me anxiously, "What if the Rockshine doesn't like me? What if it is *evil*?"

I wasn't sure something as brown and lumpy as a Rockshine could be evil, but I soothed him anyway. "Just remember the Unicorn babies. The Rockshine will need you too! Your job is to make it feel safe here in a strange place."

"I have a job?!" Regent Maximus whinnied. He tossed his head gloriously, and for a moment, he reminded me an awful lot of the Unicorns at the show. I was happy to see it. He would always be a little different from the others, but not as different as everyone had imagined.

Outside, a trailer pulled up, and I heard *"Heeeeyyyy! Hey. Heeyyyyyyyyyyyyyy!"* Despite myself, I felt a rush of excitement. Even though I wasn't crazy about Rockshines, it was impossible not to be excited for Tomas.

He emerged from the Rockshine's stall—it was right next to Regent Maximus's, and there was a door between them that could be opened in case the two turned out to get along well—and crossed his arms. He looked a little nervous. A small collection of bubbles burst around his head, but he didn't seem to notice them. It was a sign of how far Regent Maximus had come that he didn't cringe in terror from the bubbles. Instead, he blew one of them away from him with a *phbbbbbbbt* sound of his lips. Then he flinched when the bubble popped, but still. Progress!

"Hello hello, Tomas!" Mariah Gould boomed loudly from behind her long livestock trailer. "Are you ready to take on your Rockshine?" Before Tomas could reply, she answered herself. "Of course you are; you've got strong common sense!"

She stepped from behind the trailer with a big smile on her face and her arms wrapped around . . . nothing.

Of course it was because the Rockshine had gone invisible. I hadn't realized that Tomas was getting a Rockshine small enough to be carried, but it made sense that he'd get a young one to raise himself.

She stood in front of Tomas, and Tomas stared up at the empty space in her arms with big eyes.

"Now, remember," she told him, "just like we talked about on the phone. The Rockshine is going to need a bottle once a day, just for a week. Have you named her yet?"

"Bella," replied Tomas. He added in a matter-of-fact voice, "That means *beautiful* in Spanish."

Regent Maximus and I exchanged a look.

Mr. and Ms. Ramirez huddled around a camera pointed at Tomas.

Ms. Gould said, "Have a seat, cross-legged, and I'll put her in your lap. Easy, now. She's not big, but you aren't either!"

Then she tipped the invisible thing into Tomas's lap.

"Oof! I can't tell which end is which," Tomas said, and then he yipped. A slime mark had appeared on his cheek. He'd been *licked*. Tomas laughed, and the Rockshine suddenly appeared in his arms.

She was . . . cute. Well, cute-ish. She still was brown, and lumpy, and generally shaped like a hairy toaster. But she had big, friendly eyes (even if they were pointing in slightly different directions), and they weren't even runny.

"Oh!" Tomas said happily. He hugged her neck, and Bella the baby Rockshine blinked off at the sky with something like happiness.

"I call that a happy ending," said Ms. Gould.

"HEY!" shouted Bella.

TOMAS, 84ᵀᴴ TRIDENT